Perfect Imperfect Faces

Jayne Taylor

PERFECT IMPERFECT FACES

This is a work of fiction. All of the characters, names, incidents, organizations, and dialogue in this novel are either the products of the author's imagination or are used fictitiously.

iUniverse books may be ordered through booksellers or by contacting:

iUniverse
1663 Liberty Drive
Bloomington, IN 47403
www.iuniverse.com
1-800-Authors (1-800-288-4677)

Because of the dynamic nature of the Internet, any web addresses or links contained in this book may have changed since publication and may no longer be valid. The views expressed in this work are solely those of the author and do not necessarily reflect the views of the publisher, and the publisher hereby disclaims any responsibility for them.

Any people depicted in stock imagery provided by Thinkstock are models, and such images are being used for illustrative purposes only. Certain stock imagery © Thinkstock.

ISBN: 978-1-5320-4026-9 (sc)
ISBN: 978-1-5320-4027-6 (e)

Library of Congress Control Number: 2018900070

Print information available on the last page.

iUniverse rev. date: 01/10/2018

Dedication

I would like to dedicate this book to the four, perfect imperfect faces that kept me and continue to keep me alive every day. I also want to give thanks to my dear friend Sonja for being the voice of reason and encouragement when I was too afraid to share my story.

Prologue

Another beautiful day in summer lays ahead for a twelve-year-old girl without a care in the world. Awakened by the soft kiss to her forehead by her father on his way out the door to work. The two say their goodbyes and plan a game of catch tomorrow when she gets home from the sleepover set for that evening.

Up and moving, the girl hops on her bike to meet up with friends to hit the donut shop for breakfast before swim team practice. Riding through the streets laughing and singing, the thought never crossed her mind that this day would define the rest of her life.

Practice was over and all that was left was the packing and drop off to the sleepover. It was a hot day in July, Friday the 13th, but the only superstitions she had at this age would be to wear her lucky suit for races.

The sleepover took a diversion when the family she was staying with wanted to go to dinner at their friend's house. There were kids everywhere, the dinner was loud and the home was filled with so much love, you could feel it surrounding you. After dinner, it was back to make a fort in the living room and tell scary stories. The car pulled into the garage and her friend's older brother came running out to greet everyone. The girl's mother had been trying to reach her all night and left a message to come home immediately.

The parents didn't hesitate to take her home. The car turned the corner of her block, the girl saw her brother and sister's cars out front. There wasn't time to wonder what was going on, her mother came out of the house in tears.

"There's been an accident honey. Daddy is gone. Daddy is dead."

CHAPTER 1

Poster Child of Bad Relationships

As I lay awake in my bed holding on to my father's pajamas for dear life because I was afraid I would forget what he smelled like, I thought how my life was going to turn out now that he was gone. My parents were much older when they had me and were often mistaken for my grandparents. My mother was medium height with very gray hair. She volunteered at my school as the librarian from time to time. It was a roll she was destined to play. In the beginning of her volunteer days at the school I was happy to see her because my friends and I could get away with anything as long as she was in charge. As I got a little older it became embarrassing to have my mother always lurking around the halls. I believe that did not help our mother-daughter bond. Our relationship grew even worse with more time passing after my father's accident.

The feelings I had toward my mother ended up creating one of the bad relationships in my life that was to become a great regret and unfixable. Now that I am older and a mother myself I wonder if there was something that I could have done to make things better. Unfortunately, it's too late now because my mother died more than twenty-one years ago.

When I was a little girl we were close, as soon as junior high hit she and I never got along again, but I thought back then it was because I was just acting out like a normal teen. I realize that my mom was sick long before I wanted to admit it, I on some level took my father's death out on her.

My Norman Rockwell life was disrupted when I was 12 and my father was killed in a horrific car crash. In an instant my life changed drastically. I lost the one person that I truly could look up to. I was always told that my father and I looked so much alike with our dark hair, dark skin, and dark eyes. After losing him, it was hard for me to look in the mirror without seeing his face. At that age, I should have been kissing a boy for the first time and sneaking into the liquor cabinet like the rest of my friends. Well, I did do those things but I also had to start taking care of myself and eventually taking care of my mom.

My dad's being ripped away from us left a huge hole in our hearts but managed to send my mother into a horrible depression that soon got the best of her by catapulting her into early onset Alzheimer's Disease. If anyone would have had a clue how to help her or me at the time I am sure that things would have been different. Instead I began to resent my mom for leaving me stranded at school when it was her turn to drive the car pool or completely forgetting my birthday because she always seemed too upset to leave her room.

Eventually, I took charge and came to the conclusion that I would have to pick up the slack around the house. I had mom drive me to the grocery store so that I could get food for the week, never to miss picking up the two things that seemed to make her a little bit happy. Pringles and Soft Batch cookies became a main staple on the grocery list.

The older I got the more resentful I became with the situation and started to withdraw from the things that I loved to do as a kid growing up. I have always loved sports but after my father was gone, I started to become a quitter. I would try things and quit before I really gave them a chance. To this day, there are very few things that I will push through instead of quitting. The only thing that gets in my way from throwing in the towel now, is plain fear.

I wish that my mother wasn't the result of my first of many bad relationships but fate played a part in how things would end between us. After taking care of her for so many years, my siblings finally decided that my mother needed to go to a doctor because things just weren't adding up. Both my sister and brother had families of their own at this time and needed to maintain focus on their own kids, which is why it was just mom and I at the family house. Believe me, I took advantage of the lifestyle the best that I could. I am not proud of my behavior, but I would challenge any young person to not act out when there were no restrictions. I was being forced into adulthood and I started to act like I was an adult accept the fact that the adult decisions I was making were very far from the right choices.

Before my mother was diagnosed with Alzheimer's, and all the way until the end, we would fight. We fought about everything until I would stomp off and she would go right back to hiding in her room. Even when we found out she truly was sick, I manipulated things to my advantage. I learned at an early age how to arrange a situation to benefit me. I wish now that I had some of those cut-throat life skills I once had. I didn't fear consequences because to me, I had already lost my father and mother so there was nothing left to lose.

Just after my freshmen year of high school I started to date a boy who I was sure would be the beginning and end of my life. Isn't that how all teenage drama queens think at that age? I really fell for him and decided to let him be the first in what is now my skeleton closet. I believe I referred to him to my best friend, Sunny as the "founding father of my vagina". Unfortunately, Jeff's parents weren't so thrilled with his findings and demanded that we no longer see each other. A fun fact, Jeff's dad was our mailman at the time and actually had himself removed from the route to avoid me. My heart felt like someone hit me with a baseball bat in the chest. I blamed the mailman for the pain, so it is just as well he not come by my house every day.

Not so long after the break-up of the year, my mother had her driver's license taken from her by her doctors just a short time after I got my license. That meant that I became her driver instead of the other way around. Needless to say, I didn't drive her too many places because I was always so angry with her and put out by having to take care of her. That type of anger fuels fires for an attitude that won't quit.

I have been accused of being a spoiled brat, which I am pretty sure I was at the time. If I could take all of the opportunities today that were laid out in front of me when I was young, I wouldn't be trying to just survive and get by now as a middle-aged woman. I actually had a fit about the car that I was driving because it was a hand me down of my mom's and I was embarrassed driving it around. I talked her into the first of many cars that I didn't treat well and ruined.

My girlfriends and I, one of who is still what I consider to be my dearest friend, would ditch school and drive all over the place scrounging up gas money to see just how far we could push the limits. One day, the limit got pushed and left the girls and I standing on the side of the road with a smoking engine. Who knew you had to run a car with oil? I would like to say that was the first and the last time I ran a vehicle out of oil and blew an engine but it wasn't. There, in lies the spoiled brat in me. The idea of me having to make sure my cars are taken care of seemed out of this world at the time and still haunts me because I tend to second guess myself when it comes to the independence of knowing what my vehicle needs to keep running. The joys of being single and self-sufficient, I guess.

This type of behavior on my part was becoming of the norm which led to more fighting with my mother and eventually my sister who became the Power of Attorney to my mother. Talk about not wanting to answer to your older sibling! My high school years were not even close to the best years of my life and I always roll my eyes when people say that they are the best. Personally, if you feel like the choices that you make in high school constitute to your glory days then you have much to learn about adulthood and all of its roller coaster options.

Once I had gotten into a social status that I thought was the top of the food chain, my friends and I really started rebelling. One more example of me taking advantage of a really shitty situation with my mother's illness would be the never-ending parties that were held at my house every weekend. There were never any shortage of booze and drugs along with everyone from the Prom Queen to the thugs that barely even made it to school. Or at least made it to the football games to find out where the social scene would be afterwards. There might have been a moment or two where I thought this was as good as it was going to get, so I went full steam ahead. Before I knew it, I was dating upper classmen and trying out for cheerleading.

Yes, I tried out for cheerleading and actually made the squad. Back in the 80s, all of the gymnastics weren't required to fling some pom-poms around on Friday nights. Things seem to be much different now as I have watched my children go through their high school years. I never could talk my daughters into cheerleading but I did manage to get them involved in dance and gymnastics, just in case.

The celebration of making the cheerleading squad was short lived. Due to all of my excessive partying and all of the instant popularity going to my head, I found myself ineligible to participate. Imagine my surprise when the principal called me in to her office and broke the news. There are no words for the devastation of not being part of the group that I had practiced and worked so hard to get noticed by, even though my true friends were always there for me. I was told if I brought my grades up and got back on track I could try out the following year. There are only a couple of chances to try out for clubs and teams and I had completely blown it.

The shear failure of being cut should have opened my eyes to the mistakes that I was making but instead took me in a different direction. A much darker side started to emerge and become the person I was taught not to be. I am not proud of how I acted or how it shaped me as a person today, but I can honestly say I don't know where I would be if I did not learn the hard way on so many mistakes I made in the past. Going to school my junior year was the last thing that I wanted to do and for many classes, days, and weeks I just didn't attend. I was always around because I would need to see my friends or the boy that I would have a crush on for the moment. Again, things were so different then they are in this day and age. It is very hard to get away with anything now, back then if you knew when the attendance secretary was going to call, you simply had your friend answer as if she was your parent or took the phone off of the hook. Eventually, the busy signal would be just infuriating enough to give up on making the call. The movie Ferris Bueller's Day Off might have been events that I had lived or a road map on how to get away with the things I wanted to do.

I did not have many boyfriends in high school but I did have a lot of boys that were friends. I had one friend in particular that was always there for me, I considered him one of best friends. We never dated but he did go out with a bunch of my friends and I went out with a couple of his. This person was part of my group that had my back and didn't judge me, I didn't think anyway. In high school everyone judges everyone and I am not better or different than anyone else when it comes to judging. Little did I know so many decades ago having this friendship would be such a major part of my life today.

I think I first started to be interested in the "bad boys" when I got the attention of an older guy who was very into body building. So much into body building that he not only was on the five-year plan at school but also competed. The number of steroids that were used to make him a success was disturbing and fascinating all at the same time. I am not one for needles but I did give him a shot or two on a dare. I was very involved in being a number one fan of his, always so supportive. Always so stupid is more like it. This guy had a serious girlfriend that I was unaware of for a few months. I would like to sound like a stand-up kind of person and say if I would have known before going out with him I never would have, but as I mentioned, I was on a dark well-traveled road. During this period of my life, I was very vulnerable and allowed people to treat me horribly which became a pattern for many years.

Once I found out about the girl, I was already knee deep in emotions and neediness. I continued to see him regardless and got more involved in his extended group of friends that never meshed with my true friends. I lost a lot of friends this way but went based on quality as opposed to quantity. I still base my friendships on quality but I do think that you can never have too many friends, as long as they are real friends, that is.

The other girl (or was I the other girl?) found out about me and was not having any of this two-timing stuff. I can hardly blame her, but God was she a bitch. That only made me want to be around him more. How does a well-mannered Catholic girl turn into such a demon in a matter of years? I am not sure how or even when but I absolutely mastered and accepted the challenge of being the bigger bitch.

My constant desire to be defiant to any and all rules drove me to a new crowd of people. Some of these people would become the part of an even larger scale of bad relationships and many regrets. I was so determined to undermine my family that I became infatuated with one person who would change the course of my life.

My infatuation did not happen overnight. It took a while for me to come around to seeing myself with who is now my ex-husband. Back in the day of mean girls, before any pop culture movies were made about the subject, I had my own little group of mean girls to hang out with. If you can believe it, we are all student council and FBLA (Future Business Leaders of America) type people. That is beside the point, we were still mean. My ex-husband thought he would test the waters with all of these girls at one time or another.

The first girl, I will refer to her as Sandy, fell hard for Mark. We did a lot together and I watched him walk all over her, along with having another girlfriend on the side that we all knew about. If I wanted to stay true to the story her name would be Sandy as well because they both had the same name. Mark isn't terribly smart so picking a couple of girls with the same name must have made his life more manageable. Mark broke my friend Sandy's heart and moved on to the next girl in the group.

Marissa was athletic and involved in every group that she could put on a college application. Much better than the likes of Mark but still she fell for him. It did not take him long to get bored with Marissa and set his sights on Marissa's best friend Annie. Marissa landed on her feet and in Mark's brother's bed. It was meant to be a slap in the face but backfired because the two brothers didn't have a problem trading off. Marissa put up with Mark's brother for quite a while even when she found out he also had not only a very serious girlfriend but a son as well. But, this story isn't about Marissa, she married up and lives in the burbs with her wonderful family.

Poor Annie was at the bottom of the roster, I am not sure what that made me. The last to get picked for the team I guess. Annie also strived for greatness in athletics and academics. It only took a couple of dates for her to figure out it wasn't worth her time or efforts with Mark. Somehow, even though Annie figured out there were better things out there, Mark managed to kick her to the curb before she could get a word in edgewise.

After the shrapnel of girls got together, a plan was devised. It was sinister but didn't play out the way it should have. If only I would have stuck to the damn plan.

CHAPTER 2

The Plan

The plan was fairly simple, I would go out with Mark and get him to fall for me, then I would dump him. How hard can that be? Everything was going according to plan, I went to a party with Mark. The party was packed with upper classmen and red solo cups. Mark and I ended up having such a good time that he decided to come over to my house the next day to hang out. Mark lived around the block from me so it was easy just to pop over unannounced. People used to do that all of the time, now unannounced visits along with land lines and pagers are a thing of the past. Operation destroy Mark was under way, or at least the beginning stages. The girls and I just wanted to destroy his heart and maybe his reputation.

I went out with Mark a couple of times and it seemed like things were working the way my friends and I had hoped. Mark was showing a lot of interest in me and was actually being very attentive. That was the beginning of the glitch in our plan. I started to like the attention I was being shown. I realized that Mark had Sandy in his life but I didn't seem to care. I hated being home so to be out with him and all of his friends was very appealing at the time. When I was at home, he would come over and help my mom and I with things we couldn't or wouldn't do, like yard work or changing the oil in the car. I was relieved to be getting a bit of a break from the constant nagging of my mom to get things fixed or finished that I happily accepted his help. Looking back, I see I really paid for making the decision to blow off the plan and keep seeing Mark.

After a few weeks, my friends started to see I had gone in a different direction then what we had originally discussed. Everyone was mad at me for being with Mark. Not only were the mean girls pissed at me, but my other girlfriends were starting to become irritated with the amount of time I was spending, either chasing Mark or being with him. I didn't see how he was gradually making me into an insecure girl who was becoming dependent on his attention and time. I was in constant competition with Sandy for his time and ended up being on some type of a revolving door schedule. I wasn't working after school so I would go to Mark's house for a few hours, then he would send me home. It took me a while to figure out that after I would leave his house, Sandy would come over and stay the night.

I had to enlist the help of my friends, Sunny and Karrie to figure out just how badly I was being played. It was fairly routine for the three of us to jump in one of our cars and stake out the guys that we liked. We alternated cars so that we would not be so easily spotted. I think we were under the impression that we were Charlie's Angels saving the world by stocking dirt bags that were crushing hearts left and right. I can't even begin to count how many times we actually busted the guys having other girls over. When I say busted I mean we saw it happening but didn't do anything about it. There was always that moment where we were done with our so-called boyfriends and we wouldn't stand for their cheating ways. Tears, anger, and our parents' liquor cabinets usually fixed everything. Before you knew it, we were spending time with the boys, without so much as a word of how we were scorned.

This went on forever or so it seemed at the time. Sunny, Karrie and I actually drove all the way to Winter Park in a snow storm to crash the senior ski trip one year just to catch Mark in the act. All that happened was a lot of partying and a wicked hangover. The day after we got to the mountains, Karrie decided she needed to go home. So, like any good friend who was crazy for a dude, we drove home. Karrie actually drove and then dropped Sunny and I off at home. It took about five minutes for us to look at each other and throw our hands in the air as if to say, "What the hell, let's go back up the hill!" We did just that, we hopped in my car and once again drove through the snow to get to the biggest party of the season. It was actually one of the better memories that I have of high school, not just because we were going to see Mark but because we had so much fun on our adventure that weekend just to get there. As a matter of fact, we barely saw Mark because he was always ditching me and hiding from Sandy.

After the ski trip weekend and the fun that was had, it was back to the same old routine of hanging out with Mark until it was Sandy's turn. At this point, it was obvious to everyone but me that I was becoming a devoted after thought. I spent much of my time fighting to keep Mark in my life by always doing nice things for him. I not only spent much of my time, but much of my money on things Mark wanted and couldn't afford. If I had every penny that I ever wasted on him and so many other men, I would be writing this book at my house on my private island! Or at least in my condo by the beach. Mark was more than happy to accept all of my tokens of appreciation and continued to take me for what he could.

The shit hit the fan that Christmas when I found out Mark gave Sandy a ring. I got a necklace with a pearl and a diamond, but no ring. I threw a temper tantrum. A day later I received matching earrings, but no ring. It turns out that his mother bought the jewelry for both Sandy and I. I am not sure which is more disgusting, the fact that his mother bought the gifts or that she condoned his having multiple girlfriends. I was devastated, but not enough to run as fast as I could away from Mark. I think it made me want to be with him even more. Talk about damaged goods, I am still haunted by wanting to be someone's one and only, I never want to be second best.

As time went on, I tolerated more and more of Mark's demeaning behavior. My family started to become concerned with my obsession to please Mark. My sister and her husband were becoming suspicious of Mark and were not very discrete about their feelings for him. Eventually, he would turn me against my own family. Yet another regret of mine because in the end, family is all that you can count on, nothing beats unconditional love.

Spring had sprung and I was on a spiral downward. I was doing horrible in school; my friends had given up on me because I was never around and Mark was treating me worse and worse. I had finally hit what I thought was the bottom, until I got older and hit even harder. The end of my junior year was on record as one of the worst times in my life and I had plenty of bad times prior to that year so that is saying a lot. I found out that Mark had gotten Sandy pregnant. That was the straw that broke the camel's back so to speak. I lost it, I told him that I never wanted to see him again. I was so depressed that my sister called my Grandma and Aunt to come stay with my mother and I for a few days. I am so blessed to have had both of those women as role models in my life.

The visit from my family was nice but didn't change the fact that I was heartbroken and terribly depressed. My depression became all-consuming and difficult for me to handle. I no longer cared about anyone or anything including my poor mother. I am sure that part of my feelings was based on how my mother's illness was deteriorating her memory. It is one thing to forget your kid at school but a complete other thing when you forget your kid's birthday. I had enough of everything and one day came home from school and took a bunch of pills that I stole out of my mom's bathroom. I lay down on her bed and shut my eyes. As much as my mom had lost her sense of reality, she knew enough to try to save me. I woke up in the hospital to several doctors standing over me shoving a tube full of charcoal down my throat. Spoiler alert, I am still here today, so my feeble act of offing myself was unsuccessful.

Once I was released from the hospital, I was forced to go back home and deal with demons that had not gone anywhere but only seemed more terrifying. In order to avoid being committed to a psychiatric ward I had to agree to therapy. Dr. Benson was now one of my closest friends. As sad as that sounds, he was truly the only person at that time in my life who understood how I was feeling. Or at least he was getting paid to understand. I looked forward to our sessions because I could be myself and was not judged. Dr. Benson always said what I wanted to hear. I am no doctor but I am not sure if that is the best way to help someone in such turmoil. My mother came to a couple of visits with me because, like everyone else that lands in the shrink's office, she was part of the need for therapy. I hated having her there but the doctor thought it would be helpful for me to let her know how I was feeling in a space that was a safe place. The problem with me hashing out my feelings to my mother was like a weight being lifted off of my shoulders. Until we would go home and mom would forget the whole conversation. It was maddening to think I was being heard only to have my words completely erased as if the discussion never happened. Dr. Benson finally caught on to the fact that having my mom come to sessions to help me wasn't helping at all but doing more damage.

My therapy sessions went on for over a year, but my mother never was invited back in the room. The doctor and I had to come up with other ways to decrease my sadness and destructive nature. The amount of sessions became less and less productive because I had figured out that I could manipulate Dr. Benson into going along with just about anything I requested. For example, I was sure a new car would help me feel better. It took about two appointments for me to talk Dr. Benson into calling my mother to suggest taking me to get a new car. The call worked, a day later I was driving in my new red Jeep Wrangler. All of a sudden, things started to fall into place again in my social atmosphere. My friends were in my life more and Mark even came by to see me. I was working hard to recover from the mess I had made with my grades so I could graduate on time. I even entertained the idea of trying out for cheerleading again.

Things were getting more tolerable for sure. It was my senior year and I was going to go out with a bang. I picked up a bunch of extra credit to recover lost credit that put me behind and practiced for try outs every night with a girl that I used to go to grade school and be in girl scouts with. Just about a week before try outs, I got sucked back into the attention Mark was giving to me. I was told that he and Sandy were no longer together and there was not the threat of parenthood for him any longer. Mark was already out of school and working for his father with his brother Steve. He hated living at home and offered to help out around the house again if he could stay at my house. I was sure this was a turning point for us and I was more than happy to have the help and companionship because it was always so lonely being home with my mother who never came out of her room.

Before I knew it, Mark was all settled in and making himself at home. I was sure my sister would flip her lid, so I tried to hide the fact that he was actually living with us. I was able to pull that off for a while because anytime my mom would try to spill the beans I would point out to my sister how mom is barely making sense these days. My sister bought it for the time being because she had her own issues at home trying to work and raise kids. The last thing that she needed was drama from me. I was all set to go to cheerleading tryouts when Mark laid down an ultimatum. If I tried out for cheerleading he would be moving out of the house. Mark was not going to have any girl of his flaunting her ass around on the football field because it was disgraceful. I called Lisa who I had been practicing with for weeks and told her that I had a change of heart. Lisa never spoke to me again and I never looked back.

That was an extension of the treatment that would only become worse as time went on. I continued to work on my schooling because I knew I needed to get that diploma. I still had hopes of going to college. I had such high hopes for the best senior year ever, especially after such a miserable junior year. There was party after party every weekend. I was not able to go to any of the party's because Mark felt that it was not appropriate for me to be out till all hours of the night with random people. However, that didn't stop Mark from going to the party's. I would wait up half the night watching American Gladiators waiting for the door to open and Mark to come home. Half the time I was already asleep on the couch with the remote in my hand, the other half I would already be eating a bowl of cereal still waiting for him. Mark would come home whenever he wanted completely smashed with hickies all over his neck. Just writing this has me cringing at the idea that I tolerated him, but I did and I have to live with that the rest of my life.

One day in late fall, Mark told me his brother Steve needed a ride to motor vehicle and that I needed to take him. I did whatever Mark asked so I picked up his brother. Mark didn't want to go because he and a bunch of his friends were drinking and getting high so he stayed back. I failed to mention that Mark was always a pot head which I never understood, nor did I partake in. I was one of those kids that couldn't be peer pressured into doing drugs but you could sure put a drink in my hand. It was one of the things I hated about Mark but overlooked. Anyway, the motor vehicle department took hours to get through. Steve and I managed to roll into the party house about six hours after we left. Mark was furious at how long it took and accused Steve and I of not going to take care of his driver's license but instead was sure that we had snuck off and slept together. Steve and Mark started arguing and I tried to stick up for myself. Before I could even blink, Mark punched my windshield and shattered it and then turned and head butted me right in the middle of my face. Blood flew everywhere spilling out of my nose uncontrollably. I was so afraid that I was going to get hit again that I jumped in the jeep and drove off leaving the brothers there standing in the middle of the road. The first place that I went for help was to Mark's parents. I walked in the door of their house caked in blood without them even batting an eye at my horror. Mark's mom, Elizabeth didn't bother to glance up from watching tv and casually asked what happened. I explained the whole day to her and Mark's dad without any amount of sympathy from either. Both parents insinuated that I must have done something to cause Mark's outburst and that their sons better not still be fighting. At that moment, I realized that I would never be welcome or part of this family.

I was lost as to what to do about my nose because it was a mess, so I had to do what I have been and will always do when I am in trouble. I called my sister in tears. It only took her about 10 minutes to get to the house to see how bad I was. I am lucky because she works for an Ear, Nose, And Throat doctor and was able to get me in right away to have my nose re-set. I explained to her that I got into a fight with a girl at school. I was already so misbehaved that the story was certainly believable.

Mark came home the next morning after he had sobered up to see how I was and to apologize. I was told that he would never hurt me like that again. I believed him, not because I thought he was telling the truth but because I wanted to believe that someone who supposedly loves me would never want to hurt me. I forgave him and continued the story of the fight at school when asked by his family during Thanksgiving Dinner at his grandmother's house. It was a lie that I was willing to live with because I didn't want to upset Mark due to fear and shame. The shame of being a victim. The only ones who knew the real truth didn't say a word, I imagine for the same reasons.

Thank goodness, the holidays came and went without any more physical altercations and before I knew it, a new year was starting. The year that I would finish high school and start college just as my parents had hoped. I worked very hard at my grades and got a job at the mall making extra money because it was getting harder to ask my mom for money. My mom always had cash in her purse and all I had to do was ask. The past few months she started having less and less cash so it was not so easy to get my hands on. I didn't mind the job, I got a discount at the store where I got a bunch of my clothes and I had a little cash in my pocket. Until Mark took it, which was all of the time. My mom had given me a credit card that seemed to have no limit. This was not helping me manage money and would end up being a tough lesson to learn when I truly got out on my own.

Before I realized how fast time went by, spring break was coming up. Mark and I had not been getting along lately but I remained ever afraid of having my face relocated again. One day I called my childhood friend Gina who lived in Los Angeles. I told her that I was losing my mind at home and was sick of dealing with all of my problems. I never could get a good handle on dealing with things when they got hard. My sessions with Dr. Benson had become less and less and eventually I stopped going. I should have continued to see him to learn coping skills. Instead, I took that unlimited credit card and ran away from home. California…here I come.

CHAPTER 3

California or Bust

A nyone who has ever met me or knows me is aware that I absolutely love California. My brother moved out to San Diego shortly after my father passed away. My mother started sending me out to visit without her for every break and holiday that she could just to get some peace and quiet. Mostly just so she wouldn't have to deal with me. I did not argue, it only took one trip out to Cali to realize that I belong there. I may have been born in Colorado but I should be a California native.

It makes perfect sense for me to want to run away to a place that I love so much. I was fortunate to have my friend Gina living in Los Angles at the time I needed an escape. It would have been foolish to head to my brother's. That would be the first-place people would look for me. By people I mean Mark. He had started to become dependent on me as much as I was depending on him. In other ways like funding his addictions or making sure dinner was done as opposed to my dependency of help with the yard work and plumbing.

I called Gina with my itinerary so I would have a way to her place from the airport, I was very good at traveling alone because of all of the trips my mother had sent me on earlier. However, this time I wouldn't be under the watchful eye of some nosey flight attendant

18

which was refreshing. I am used to doing things without permission, no babysitter required.

Gina wasn't driving yet and her mom was about as interested in her as my mom was in me. Under different circumstances though, her mom moved away from Colorado after the divorce and my mom was just plain sick. Gina and I had been finding trouble since preschool, way before our parents flaked out on us. Then we hit our preteen years and things went south in the parenting department so we really got into some risky business. Between her mom and dad being at each other's throats and my mom's situation we managed to get away with anything we wanted and me running away was no different.

Sure, her mom knew I was coming but just figured it was all arranged by some higher power. The higher power was me in this situation. Once I arrived in LA, the fun began. In the 80s it was so much easier to be invisible because there were only land phone lines and very little terrorist threat situations. Gina and I took the bus everywhere and had the best time meeting people and being on our own personal vacation. We went to parties with the kids that Gina was in school with and hit the beach and the outdoor malls as much as two teenage girls with a credit card possibly could. I had forgotten how nice it was to look out for just me and not have to be worried about what someone else thinks of me.

About three days into the destination vacation, Gina's phone rang. Of course, we answered and without caller ID there was no way to tell who was on the other line. We were expecting a call for the next party invite but instead the voice on the other end of the phone was Mark. I had been found and I was not thrilled. Mark decided to ask my mother for her phone book and started calling all of the people that might have an idea where I would be. He actually had to make a few calls because Gina's last name starts with an M. Was this an act of desperation or just making a point that once again Mark was trying to be in control of my life? I think a little of both, he didn't want to be stuck at my place with my mom to look after nor did he want me to be doing something that was just for me.

Mark talked me into flying back home, but there were still a few days left of spring break before it was time to go back to the rat race of school and work. Somehow, I ended up begging his forgiveness for my abrupt departure. I promised to fly home, pick him up and we would jet off to Mexico for a long weekend. This was a time when no passports were needed, just a birth certificate for identification to leave the country. That is if you are over the age of 18. I was not yet 18 so I had to do a little more leg work to escape. It truly was an escape because I was not telling my family of my new travel plans. They hadn't yet had time to recover from my last trip. I had to sneak in my mom's lock box and get my father's death certificate because at that time both parents signatures were required on notarized notes giving me permission to leave the United States. I had my certificate, my dad's certificate, and a forged note that the bank notarized without my mom being present in order to catch my flight. It's odd how things were so easily processed without question. Its people like me that create a need for all of the legal red tape that we go through today just to take a vacation.

Mark and I flew to Puerto Vallarta shortly after I returned from California. As much as I wanted to stay in California and never go back to Colorado, Mexico was a good follow up without a doubt. Palm trees, sand, and unlimited cocktails. We hiked in the jungle, took jeep tours, and lounged on the beaches during the day. At night we would go into the town and check out the nightlife. A girl could get used to this and Mark was relaxing and having fun. Almost to the point that I thought he was a good boyfriend and wouldn't ever hurt me again. We were out of our regular element surrounded by strangers and paradise. We were the happiest that we had ever been and it gave me hope that when we got back home things would be better.

The last night of our trip we decided to hit the clubs again. We had met some Americans from South Carolina. Charlie and Cindy were on their first anniversary celebration trip and were just as happy to hang out with us as we were to hang out with them. None of us were remotely fluent in Spanish and my French classes did not seem to be helping my ability to communicate. Charlie and Mark decided to leave Cindy and I at Carlos O'Brien's while they ran to the hotel we were all staying at to get more cash. We would only carry little amounts of cash because we were afraid that the locals would try to rob us. A couple of hours went by and I started to get freaked out. I wasn't old enough to be down there by myself let alone trying to find Mark. Cindy was starting to get worried about the boys too so we decided to try to call the hotel. The hotel had no idea who Mark and Charlie were nor were they able to pinpoint them returning or leaving the hotel at any specific time. Just as I was about to start crying because that is how I react to everything, Mark and Charlie walked through the door.

They told us how they were approached by some girls that were asking for money but would happily trade for sexual favors. My tears turned to anger because our track record has never been good, I immediately assumed that Mark took them up on their offer. I may never know what really happened that night but Charlie assured Cindy and I that not only were these girls working for the police, but shortly after they were approached, the police came out and tried to arrest them. In Mexico if you have money on you it is very easy to get out of anything. Charlie and Mark gave the police all of the money they had on them and were released. Do I believe the story? It no longer matters, I was fearing more for myself and my safety so I was relieved that Mark was back in my sights. Fortunately, Mark and Charlie never reached the hotel to get more cash only to be cleaned out.

We finished out our night laughing and drinking and dancing on the bar. Charlie and Cindy were staying a few days longer then us but we exchanged addresses and phone numbers to keep in touch. I was young and foolish and didn't realize once we left them that night at the bar we would never hear from them again. That is the way the world works, you meet what you think will be life-long friends and travel companions when you are on vacation without a care in the world. Then you get back on the plane and reality slaps you in the face upon landing.

Mark and I returned late Sunday night, just in time to do a load of laundry and get ready for school the next day. I was on the downhill push to complete high school which I had come to hate more than ever. Before I knew it, it would be time for prom and then graduation. No one in my family even questioned what I had been doing. It felt like I got away with something fantastic and it felt deviously delicious. I vowed to take a trip like that at least once a year for the rest of my life. What a joke that is, as an adult the unlimited credit limit is not real. Eventually, my big vacation heist was found out about by my sister. Stupid credit card statement! As the power of attorney over my mother's finances the bills were redirected to Terry's house. I remember how furious Terry was with me spending so much of our mother's money. At the end of the day, Terry might have been in charge of mom but she damn sure wasn't in charge of me. Power of attorney over finances is clearly not the same thing as being guardian and I was almost 18. There was really nothing that could be done accept a bunch of yelling and screaming. I had become immune to that type of noise a long time ago and wasn't going start paying attention to it now.

There went the feeling of relaxation from the vacation. Mark resumed his old ways shortly after we got home. He jumped into the role of control freak and I slipped right back into submissive pushover. The only thing I had to look forward to was Senior Prom, A Night to Remember. That was the lame theme of the prom. I am not even sure if that is a theme or just what Student Council was calling the event. I was no longer in Student Council because Mark said it was taking up too much of my time after school. After all, who was going to make dinner after a hard day of work if I was sitting in a classroom planning social events?

Our Prom was set on a Friday and the after-prom party was to be held at a place called Fun Plex. I spent much of my junior high school weekends at Fun Plex. It had everything a kid could want. Roller skating, dancing, video games, junk food, the absolute best place to meet your friends without parental supervision. Because I had messed up so much in my previous years at school, I was limited to the number of classes that I was able to miss. I had one history teacher who was on to my ways and told me and my girlfriends that he would fail us if we did not show up the day of prom for his class. Silly Archuleta, I scheduled my nail and tanning appointment to be during algebra, went to history class and then left to get my hair done. All he did was piss me off because he was cutting into my prep time. I still managed to look like the little mermaid in my very sequined white and silver off the shoulder skin tight prom dress. It was simply gorgeous and made me feel like a princess.

Prom was a very memorable time in the four years that seemed to go on forever. All of my friends went together on one giant date and then to the after-prom party. We played every game and managed to have fun without being totally smashed. There was a wedding chapel set up that I insisted on visiting with Mark. He indulged my childhood fantasy, we got in line to be faux married. That was the first of three times I would make that mistake with him. The other two times had more paperwork and seemed to stick more than the bubble gum machine ring that was provided that night.

Another fun filled night in the books spent with my favorite people. My friend Karrie was dating one of Mark's best friends at the time so it was easy to get to hang out with her minus any drama of me spending too much time with Mark. Karrie and Craig dated for a few months and really seemed to hit it off. The next thing we had to look forward to was graduation. I was close to hitting my credits but would not be sure until the last week of school. Talk about timing, there were so many events to attend. I went to all of the senior events even if I ran the risk of not walking because I wasn't going to miss out on everything due to lack of a small piece of paper. First on the list of events, senior ditch day. I only attended half of that party due to good ol' history class. Then came the senior brunch minus mimosas which is now a must if the word brunch has been brought to my attention. The week of graduation came and low and behold, I had just enough credits to walk with my class. All of the seniors loaded up on the buses that had taken us so many places over the last few years and created what I now know to be lasting memories. The buses took us to the Denver Coliseum which smelled like ass. A livestock show had been hosted there a few weeks before and it truly smelled like ass, as in horse, cow, donkey you name it. Our high school usually had graduation at the outside venue up in Morrison called Red Rocks. It is such a beautiful place that I have seen many concerts and graduations at over my lifetime. The year I graduated it was under renovation so we got to follow up the animals.

I was still not 18 and thought I was awesome because I had worked so hard to get to where I was and did it before I was a true adult. It was all in the timing of my birthday but it didn't matter to me. My whole family or what was left of them came and helped celebrate by making a huge dinner and a party after the ceremony. Mark's family also attended and had gotten used to the idea of us being together, even though they always truly loved Sandy. As time went on, Sandy's broken heart healed and the bitch actually found a catch. I cared then, I don't care now. It doesn't hurt that she hasn't aged well.

There were several parties to visit of all of the people that graduated and I went to all of them because when you are the star of your own show, you don't take the time to realize that the people who came together to celebrate with you actually want you to be there and not just a figment of their imaginations. I know that I was being selfish but it was my day and I chose to spend it party hopping. When the parties came to an end and life was getting back to semi normal with me getting up and heading to work every day, I started to think about what was next to come.

My 18th birthday was shortly after graduation so there was a bit more partying to be done. Mark and I were back into a rut of struggling to like each other. Steve was tired of living at home with his parents so he asked Mark if we wanted to get a condo with him. I thought this would be a great way to jump into adulthood. Our living arrangements lasted about three weeks. It was hard enough to live with Mark but when you add his brother to mix it was a recipe for disaster.

I couldn't take it anymore, I called my friends and they helped me move the things that I had over at the condo back home. Mark ended up staying at my house more than he was at the condo but I didn't care. I could do whatever I wanted at home and not pay rent so there was no need for me to be out of the house. Steve and Mark used to have parties all of the time at the condo but I stopped going because it was always the same people all stoned and sitting around staring at each other. My friend Karrie had met someone else when we were cruising around Evergreen one night and had lost interest in Mark's friend Craig. That was a bummer for Craig and me because it meant neither of us got to hang out with Karrie. Craig was heartbroken and kept asking me to fix things between him and Karrie. I wanted them to be together but I had seen how happy Karrie's new friend made her and I couldn't interfere with what was then and still is the love of her life.

One hot summer night in July around midnight, I got a call from Mark. He was drunk and wanted to come to my house because his brother wasn't shutting the party down anytime soon. I jumped in the jeep and headed over to pick him up. I offered to give a few other people a lift too because I had not been drinking and those guys were toast. As ridiculous as this sounds since I just stated my sobriety at the time, I let Mark drive. He insisted and I rarely argued with him for obvious reasons. Mark was driving, I was sitting in the middle right over the stick shift and Craig was in the passenger seat. In the back we had a kid we called Milk because he looked like the little boy on the "Got Milk" commercial from the 80s. The other passenger was a good buddy of Mark and me. It was a full load and spirits were high accepting Craig. He was high all right, Craig dabbled in hard core drugs and probably had an addiction problem with drugs and alcohol. A part of the reason that Karrie was separating herself from him. Craig was almost in tears and as Mark was driving and the kids in the back were laughing and singing, Craig looked at me and said he couldn't take it anymore and opened the jeep door. I grabbed his arm as he flew out but couldn't hold on to him. Mark slammed on the breaks and everyone sobered up very fast. We jumped out to find Craig lying unresponsive in the middle of the road. Milk gave him mouth to mouth to try to get him to start breathing. Once that wasn't working the guys picked Craig up and put him in the back seat of the jeep. We were covered in blood and scared out of our minds. Milk and Dave walked to the apartment that Craig shared with his best friend Tim to let him know what was happening and to call Craig's parents. Mark and I drove as fast as we could to get help. Our first thought was to get Craig to the hospital but when we were driving we spotted a police officer. Mark stopped the jeep and ran over to get help. The officer called for an ambulance and then started questioning us as to what had happened. It sure seemed like we were trying to do the right thing and didn't think we would be to blame, but that is exactly what happened.

The ambulance arrived and got Craig out of the jeep, then rushed to the hospital. The police officer made Mark and me get in his car to follow the ambulance. The air was so thick you could slice it with a knife if you wanted to. The heat and the terror were getting to both Mark and I as we sat in the back of the cop car. The windows were not able to be rolled down and there were no handles to escape as if there were somewhere for us to go. The officer told Mark he would need to take a blood test for suspicion of alcohol. He kept asking, "How much did your friend have to drink tonight? "Neither of us answered because we didn't really have any idea what Craig had been ingesting.

We arrived at the hospital still covered in one of our dear friend's blood only to have Mark carted off in handcuffs. I was left there to face Craig's parents when a doctor came into the waiting room and said that they did everything they could. Craig was gone, he never survived the initial fall and Mark and I were in trouble.

CHAPTER 4

Cheap Sunglasses and Small Karats

Cheap Sunglasses by ZZ Top was blaring as we walked into the funeral home for Craig's service. It was an odd but appropriate choice because it was one that Craig played constantly. I wasn't sure if Mark or I would be able to attend for several reasons. Mark had just been bailed out of jail for the DUI. He ended up serving five days in the county jail before he was released. Neither one of us was welcome by the family. As a parent now, I understand the need to blame someone for the misfortunes that happen to your children. Craig's parents were trying to say that I pushed Craig out of the jeep and attempted to press charges. They also blamed Mark for driving under the influence and felt that was part of the reason the accident happened. The accident was heavily investigated by the police and was ruled to be nothing more than a tragic accident. The parents and sister of Craig still blamed us and would blame us for the rest of their lives.

The funeral was short and terribly sad because of how young Craig was when he died. In the coming weeks, Mark sunk into a deep depression. The loss of such a close friend is hard for anyone but when you are having to relive the loss for each court appearance it becomes even harder. I tried to help him get past the grief but nothing was working. I was so desperate, I put my hatred and insecurities to the side and called Sandy. I was willing to do whatever I could to get Mark help, so was Sandy. She came to visit Mark and he asked me to leave so they could talk. I was hurt but if that was going to help him get through his pain, so be it. Nothing came of their talk other than Mark feeling a little better about his situation and his sadness where Craig was concerned.

Mark had already served the amount of time the courts sentenced him to for the violation and had to do community service hours and pay a fine. I am always baffled at how Mark is able to get away with doing as little as possible when it comes to the law. His community service was done at a gym that he went to everyday to work out. The manager signed off on all of Mark's hours as if he were doing some great service but he really was just doing what he normally does. The fines were paid by his parents who took pity on the outcome of the accident. The case was closed which allowed Mark to move past the last couple of months. Only to return to his previous selfish ways.

Before I had time to decompress from all of the events over the summer, it was time for me to go back to school. I had no desire to go to school anymore but I knew it was in my plan and would help me in the future. My friend Karrie and I got checks from our mothers and went to the local community college to enroll in classes. We signed up for core classes because we had no clue what to be when we grew up. I am still trying to figure that out.

The first class we attended was English 101. I had always been good at English so I was sure this would be a breeze. The only thing that was a breeze about that particular professor or class was when we asked for a refund. The class was hard and Karrie and I were quick to give up on going. I think we went about three weeks before we went to the registration office to get our money back. The one thing that I remember was an overwhelming sense of failure and I wasn't going to continue to set myself up to fail. The school refunded us the money for all of the classes that we had signed up for but the checks were made out to us, not our parents. We did what any 18-year-old girls with a check in hand would do, we went shopping.

Then continued the facade of being students for a few more weeks and met up for breakfast or just goofed off. This gave me time away from Mark and Karrie kept her folks off her back. It was much easier for me to maintain the illusion of going to school. Karrie's parents were on to her and made her get a full-time job to pay them back. My life was getting ready to take a turn but not in the employment department.

After the cover was blown about quitting school something much bigger happened. I got pregnant. I suspected for a few weeks but was too afraid to really find out. One Saturday morning, I called and asked Karrie to come over and lend moral support while I took the test. It was positive and now I had to deal with the consequences. I was petrified to tell Mark, especially how he handled the pregnancy with Sandy. I was not going down that road, so I was preparing myself for a fight.

Mark was staying with me again because he wasn't making enough money to support his habits and pay rent. I wasn't sure if I should ask Karrie to stay while I told him or if I should just suck it up and give him the news alone. I did both, Karrie went in the basement while I told Mark upstairs in the living room. She was hanging around to make sure I was going to be okay. There was no fighting, Mark accepted the idea of being a father and actually embraced the news. I was shocked about his reaction but relieved at the same time.

I was not ready to deal with how my family would react to the news and was not showing off a baby bump so I elected not to say anything for the time being. A few days after I found out about my pregnancy we had dinner with Mark's whole family. I remember sitting there hoping they would not figure anything out until I was ready to drop the bomb. That night my thunder was stolen, Mark's brother Steve and his girlfriend the mother of his first child unloaded the news of them having another baby that would be arriving in June. Mark and I looked at each other in disbelief. Two seconds later Mark told the family our news. These people were so odd, they started laughing. All of them thought it was a joke about us having a baby. I didn't think it was any laughing matter but whatever floats their boat. Our baby wasn't due until late July so they all had time to absorb the family growing and taking us seriously.

Weeks went by and I finally had to tell my family about the baby. The initial reaction was one of pure disappointment. My mom told me not to expect her to babysit because she had done enough of that for my brother and sister's kids. Not to worry, she was way beyond being capable of taking care of babies. As power of attorney for my mother, Terry thought she would teach me a life lesson and take me off of mom's insurance plan. I was told to figure it out on my own because I was an adult making adult choices. Mark did not have medical insurance because his dad was self-employed and paid Mark and Steve out of pocket.

I had to have medical care, so I went through a local hospital that accepted small payments to work toward the doctor visits and hospital bill. This was not a terrific option but it did help when we had no insurance and no money. The sad thing is the life lesson that was deemed on me was just another thing to add to my list of adult responsibilities that I had been dealing with from the age of 12.

Just before Christmas, Mark, myself and his whole family traveled to Chicago for a family wedding. I was showing by then but never really got sick so I was good to travel. The trip was fun and the wedding was gorgeous. After the wedding was over Mark and I went back to his Uncle's house because I was exhausted and Mark was loaded. I kept going on and on about the wedding and how lucky the cousin was to be married. In a drunken state, Mark proposed. It wasn't glamourous or even romantic, it was more like," Do you want to get married or what?" Of course, I immediately accepted because the idea of raising the baby outside of marriage was not what I wanted. I had always had dreams of having the happy family that I once had with my parents before the shit hit the fan. I was determined to create that Norman Rockwell picture perfect life and nothing was going to get in my way.

The family went back to Colorado after the wedding just in time for Christmas. Mark and I announced our engagement and set a date for early April to make sure the baby would be born after the wedding. There was so much to plan in such a short time but I didn't care. This was going to be my day where I would be the center of attention. The proposal left little to be desired and there once again was no ring so the first order of business was to go to the jewelry store and pick one out. I picked a small princess cut diamond set on a gold band with a wrap-around wedding ring. The diamond in the band and the six diamonds in the wedding ring did not even equal a karat. That was all that I could afford because Mark didn't have any money and said he would help pay back the credit card that I applied for to get the rings. I am sure that never happened but was happy to have the rings that I had been wanting for over two years. Mark was not willing to wear a ring, for the ceremony we purchased him a cheap band. I was told his work was too dangerous to be wearing jewelry but in reality, he was worried about his outwardly appearance to other women.

My family was on board with the wedding because of our Catholic upbringing and not having a baby out of wedlock. As the bride it was our duty to pay for the reception and the grooms duty according to all of the wedding magazines to pay for the rehearsal dinner. Mark and I were the first to be married out his siblings and his mother wanted something special. My sister, Grandma and Aunt had planned for us to be married in a non-denomination church because Mark's family was Baptist and the Catholic Church would not marry us without Mark converting. He isn't religious but his mother was not about to allow Mark to become Catholic. The family would then all pitch in and make food for a reception to be held at my mom's house. I thought it would be perfect but Mark's mother, had other ideas.

We found a nice church that was decorated completely in

versions of pink. My favorite color and the color that I had picked for my bridesmaids. My wedding dress was also a very faint shade of pink covered in lace and ruffles. It was the most amazing dress I had ever seen and I had to have it for my big day. My head piece was one that would be pinned into my hair and was very heavy once the train was attached. The train itself was 25 feet, this was back when every little girl watched the Royal Wedding of Charles and Di and needed to have a train that was as long as a football field.

Elizabeth was satisfied with the church, thank goodness. I am not sure what would have happened if she didn't get the wedding she had dreamed of for her precious son. However, there was no having a reception in someone's backyard in her book. Elizabeth started researching hotel ball rooms and catered meals. This idea of a wedding was out of our budget no matter how much money my mother actually had in her savings account. Mark's parents said they would pay for the wedding reception if my family took care of the rehearsal dinner. My sister Terry jumped on that idea quickly to save mom the money.

The joke was on Elizabeth because my family made all of the food and had the rehearsal dinner at mom's house. Everyone went to the church while the family members that were not involved in the wedding stayed home and set up for the meal. I had my niece and nephew as the flower girl and usher. They were the oldest at the time and were the only ones that would take any direction. Mark's nephew was the ring bearer. The children were adorable but they were the only family members I had in my wedding with the exception of my Uncle walking me down the aisle. I was so mad at my sister half the time that I didn't want her to be in the wedding. It was my way of teaching her a life lesson in my own passive aggressive way.

Mark's whole family was somehow a part of the wedding but he wasn't going to have it any other way. I had to have his two sisters who I would compare to as wicked step sisters as my bridesmaids along with a couple of my friends. Karrie was my maid of honor because Gina could not fly in from California for the wedding.

After the rehearsal dinner was over, the family started cleaning up and then heading home to prepare for the next day. Mark had it set to stay at his parent's house because of my superstitious nature of not wanting the groom to see the bride until the day of the wedding. I was so tired I went to bed so that I could have my beauty sleep. I found out a couple of years later that Mark went to bed but not at his folk's house and not alone. It would be the last night that he spent with Sandy.

The next morning, I woke up refreshed and ready to start my day. As I had done for as many Saturdays as I could remember, I started with cartoons and a bowl of Froot Loops. What better way to kick off your wedding day? The girl who had been doing my hair for years came to the house to fix my hair and I had my nails done, it was like going to prom but more expensive. The day flew by and before I knew it, it was time to go to the church. My whole family was there, as well as half of the school. The church was simply magical and everything was going perfectly. Due to the baby coming there would not be an immediate honey moon but I didn't care because I was finally getting what I wanted, someone to take care of me for once. So, the saying goes, "be careful what you wish for".

The ceremony was quick but I had run out of steam being six months pregnant. How many pictures need to be taken at these things before a girl can eat? After we had the last picture at the church taken, we loaded up into a white Rolls Royce rented by Mark's parents. Complete with champagne for Mark and apple juice for me. We toasted the crowd and off we went to the reception a few miles away. The hotel ballroom was spectacular, I couldn't have dreamt of anything better. The food was amazing, the music was perfect for dancing and I was having the night of my life. Just as the night was winding down and everyone was saying their goodbyes, Mark's friends that were not invited showed up. There went my wedding night, right down the drain or rather up Mark's nose. He invited these people that I specifically banned up to our honeymoon suite and proceeded to get completely drunk and high while I laid in bed and cried. Thank God for that baby, I had nothing in my future to look forward to with Mark.

The night came and went and so did Mark's friends. We went to his parent's house to pick up all of the gifts that we had been given and went back to my mom's house. Once again, I was being taught a valuable lesson. Terry informed me that we would need to move out because it was her intention to sell mom's house eventually and move her into an assisted living home. I was at a loss for words. I felt every emotion one would think of when being kicked out six months pregnant and newly married.

Fortunately, it was not immediate which gave us some time to figure out where we were going to land. I believe that Terry had some reservations about moving mom into a home right away but her husband was in her head about what to do all of the time. Terry and I sat down and came up with an arrangement that was going to make everyone happy. The arrangement was for me to be Terry's day care provider at no cost and a house would be purchased for Mark and I to move into and pay rent at a low rate. I actually was willing to accept the offer because I was tired of being mom's caregiver. Instead I started taking care of three kids. Needless to say, Mark was all in favor of the move and the idea of having his own home.

A month later, we moved into our little two-bedroom home a few blocks from mom so that I would be around in case of emergency. Mark continued to work for his father making about $200 a week which was hardly enough to live off of because I was working for free and providing food for the three kids not to mention all of the money that Mark spends on his various habits. We did scrape up enough money to buy an above ground pool that was big enough for the kids to play in and me to float around on in my huge pregnant state. It was summer and I was hot and cranky so the kids and I stayed in the pool most days just for some relief.

The middle of June and it was hitting upwards of 90 plus degrees every day. One day I got a call that Mark's brother Steve had taken his girlfriend to the hospital. It was time, their time for a baby anyway. I loaded up my niece and nephews and off we went to meet the new baby. I wasn't due for 6 more weeks but after seeing that baby, I sure was ready to be done with pregnancy. The new baby boy in the family was absolutely perfect and made me all the more excited for my little boy to arrive.

The following day was a Saturday and was the day of my baby shower. Terry was throwing me a party in order to get ready for the baby complete with my craving of ice cream cake. The family was all there along with several of my friends. I wasn't feeling great but I chalked that up to being fat and tired. We played this stupid game of everyone guessing just how big my belly is by cutting a string and then making me go around the room for them to measure their string around my stomach. The last guest to measure my stomach got more than she bargained for, my water broke.

CHAPTER 5

The Golden Child

A gush of water and some mortified guests before it occurred to me that the baby would be coming. Terry jumped right into action by rushing everyone out of the house while I tried to reach Mark. He and Tim had gone fishing for the day to stay out of the way of all of the girls. It never occurred to me to have a way of contacting him in case of emergency. We still had six weeks to prepare for the baby, I didn't even have a bag packed for the hospital.

Once everyone left, my sister sent her husband to go get Mark while I tried not to panic. I called the doctor on call to find out how long I could wait before leaving for the hospital. I wasn't having contractions so I had some time to get myself together. I was scared to death, I went to a Lamaze class a few weeks earlier but none of that seemed to help the fact that I was missing my coach. Time felt like it had stopped as my sister's kids were crawling all over me like they normally would, which was making everything so much more painful. In their defense, they were just trying to help their cousin come out.

Finally, after about an hour and a half, Mark came running through the door. We did not take the time to go home and pick up my things because Terry volunteered to bring them to the hospital as soon as the baby arrived. It was about 5 o'clock when we hopped in the car and drove to the hospital. If you have ever driven down Sixth Avenue towards Downtown Denver, you would know that it is a very bumpy ride. I still wasn't having contractions but was getting more afraid by the minute.

Once we got to the hospital, I went to the front desk and tried to explain that my water broke and the baby wasn't due for a few weeks. The payment plan for the hospital was not yet paid in full because I thought that I still had time. The admissions secretary had the nerve to look at me and tell me that they could not see me until my debt was paid. At that point I started seeing red! I started screaming obscenities that I wouldn't say to my worst enemy. (Sandy..) Nothing changed the fact that this woman was trying to keep me from having my baby in the hospital until I wrote her a check. That is just what I did, bounce, bounce, bounce, but I was finally in a room.

The doctor came into to see how I was progressing and found that I was still not dilating at the rate that I should have been. He suggested that I get up and walk for a while to see if that will get things moving. Hours went by before it was finally time to start pushing. I had never felt pain like what I was experiencing and was offered a medication to be put in my IV to take the edge off. The only edge it took off was my ability to react. I could still feel all of the pain but was in a haze, it was miserable. The doctor said that I needed to push, the minute the baby was about to come out, Tim's wife came bursting through the delivery room door. Who does that? Not even my own mother was in the room with Mark and I. Mark's mother was out of town so his dad was waiting in the next room with my sister. I didn't have time to ask Amy to leave because the baby was coming. Mark was very supportive and was ready to cut the umbilical cord with the doctor's instructions. One more push and this nightmare would soon be over.

Mark was at the receiving end ready and waiting until he got pushed out of the way. Junior was born with the cord around his neck and wasn't breathing. I kept waiting to hear that precious baby cry but only heard gasps for air. Mark and I were terrified and helpless because all we could do was watch our baby struggle to breath. It was one of the most frightening times that I had ever experienced. Luckily, the doctors and nurses were on point and prepared for anything because of the premature labor. The cord was removed and Junior started screaming. His little lungs were letting out a noise that sounded like angels singing. I was the first person to hold this precious little gift with a full head of brown hair. I had seen babies before but this baby seemed to be the most perfect little person in the world and he was all mine.

The baby was named after Mark and was called Junior for about a month. I was fine with that because it was a tradition in Mark's family. My own father was named after my grandfather and was also called Junior, which made the name even more special to me.

Junior arrived at 11:38pm that Saturday in June and would change my life forever. The hospital was quick to get me and the baby out the door. We were both given a clean bill of health less than eight hours after the deliver and sent packing. You get what you pay for when it comes to medical care. I was told that a traveling nurse would be by to check on the baby within 24 hours. I did not pay for that service but because I was still technically a teenager it was automatic.

When we got home, I went into the house to find my sister's family waiting with a completely stocked nursery. I had not been home since I left the day before for the baby shower and that room was empty. I was so thankful and for the first time in a long time remembered the person that I had grown up with instead of my mother's keeper. Shortly after Terry and the kids left, Steve and his girlfriend and new baby came by for a visit. These two boys would grow up together being only three days apart. I would also have someone to talk to about what I was going through with a baby the same age. None of my friends were even close to having kids and I would soon find that my friendships would fade or drift apart. That is a tuff pill to swallow when you realize you no longer have your friends to lean on.

My youth was on my side having a baby because my sister dropped her kids off the next day so that she could go to work. No rest for the wicked or for me. The kids were so thrilled to see Junior and actually were helpful when I needed someone to grab diapers and wet wipes. It all worked out as good training for me because of the other kids that I eventually would have.

As time went on, we found that having a baby as glamorous as it may have seemed was very expensive. Mark and I were always fighting about money which would give him a reason to leave and go hang out with his friends. Mark was never around and I was taking care of the baby and the house and the two dogs that we had all alone. I had whined to Terry enough that she could no longer stand it. Her husband, Jack called Mark and offered him a job in the construction company that employed him. Mark was not thrilled, nor was his father but we needed the money and the insurance. When Mark took the call, I was out getting our groceries with the help of my mother because I would take her to the store once a week. Yet again abusing my privileges and adding an extra thing or two to my own pantry just to get by. All the more reason to take the offer.

It never once crossed my mind to get on birth control right away. I didn't want anything to do with Mark in that area so I assumed I was safe. However, just because I didn't want to sleep with Mark didn't mean I didn't have to. Mark had not hurt me physically since he broke my nose but still remained in control of our relationship that was purely based on fear and lies. I did what any wife would do in this situation, I slept with him. It was part of the job, much like doing the laundry or walking the dogs.

Summer break was over and the kids just needed before and after school care which opened up the whole day for me and the baby to do whatever I wanted. Well, as long as it applied to the "job" I referred to. It was hard for my sister's kids to say Junior so we started calling him Markie. I spelled it with an I-E at the end because I always wanted my name to be spelled that way. As a grown adult he still goes by Markie. I respect that because a lot of people drop their nicknames when they get older out of fear of judgment.

Markie was about three months old when we found out that I was pregnant again. Talk about fear of judgement, I knew both families would have something to say. Mark was thrilled because another baby meant more control over me. Anytime I got remotely independent he would figure out a way to take it away from me. Barefoot and pregnant was working for him, he would still do whatever he wanted and I would be home like some Leave It to Beaver character. For anyone reading this who is not sure what that means, Google it.

I was perfectly happy having another baby because I was so in love with Markie. I was sure that the kids would grow up to be best friends being so close in age just like Mark and Steve. They are only thirteen months apart and do everything together. Mark's family didn't have much to say as expected. It was my family that would voice their opinions on how my life was playing out. Telling mom was easy, she would forget before I walked out the door so there were no negative comments from her at the time. Terry and Jack shook their heads in disbelief but their two oldest kids are just a year and a half apart which I was quick to point out.

My brother Ted on the other hand was a challenge to get on board. We weren't very close because he is twenty years older than I am and we don't have the same father. I believe that Ted always resented me because of the difference in our parents. Our ideas of parenting were very different. Any more than one child to him was over populating the world. I am glad he had that one kid because he is one of my best friends.

Eventually, everyone got used to the idea of baby number two in our home. Mark worked out of town during the week and was home on the weekends. It was hard on him and hard on Markie and I. It was already Christmas and I was starting to become more and more exhausted taking care of all of the kids and being pregnant again. I spoiled Markie for that year that he had my attention because I knew once the next baby came along all of that would change. I knew that I was having another boy, which worked perfect for our housing situation. The baby would sleep in my room until he needed the crib and then Markie would have to move into a bed. I had it all figured out. If Mark continued working steadily we would be able to survive.

The construction business was booming. Both Mark and Jack had plenty of work to help provide for the two families. I had become more and more estranged from any of my friends which left Markie and my sister's kids to focus on. I would meet with Karrie once in a while for breakfast or lunch but that was few and far between. Karrie was now engaged and would be having a wedding about the time the baby was due, but I would be there standing by her side even if I had to have an extra few yards of taffeta and lace to cover my belly.

My spring breaks were once so exciting, now they were full of kids running around and a husband who was working nights. That was a long week because I was expected to keep all of the kids quiet and Markie was crawling and getting into everything. I was so busy doing the round up I hardly noticed how unhappy I was becoming. I chalked my feelings up to being hormonal and would feel better once the baby was here.

I helped Karrie as much as I was allowed because Mark expected me to be home when he was home. The wedding was getting closer and so was the expected arrival of Tony. Another hot summer to get through being the size of a baby elephant. The heat and the day care were starting to take its toll on me, I was having pain after pain. Two months before Tony was due I went into labor. I was rushed to the hospital, I had medication to stop the labor and was asked to be on bed rest. For about a minute of my life I thought that meant that I would get a little help from Mark and maybe my sister would not bring the kids over so much. Just for a minute did I think that though, I was quickly reminded by the request of dinner when we got home from the hospital and a crying baby. I was sure that Tony would be an independent boy because he was having to fend for himself before he was even born.

Business as usual for the next couple of weeks until I was back in the hospital in labor again. This time I took a bag, I was planning on staying until Tony arrived. No such luck, I was sent home again. We had to make it two more weeks to make sure all of Tony's organs would be developed. I tried to do the best that I could to take care of myself and I made it to the cutoff. Tony was born a tiny little peanut, three days after Markie turned one. It was a nice healthy little present for Markie.

Tony was born with fiery red hair, which was shocking to both Mark and I. If I would not have had him I would have questioned the baby being mine. The doctor explained to both of us about recessive family genes and how it is possible for a couple of brunettes to have red haired children. We took Tony home a day later weighing in at just five pounds.

If the story seems like a bit of a repeat, it's probably because it was very similar to just the year before. The new difference other than the obvious extra character is the amount of debt that our family was building. Two kids in diapers with medical bills from the births started to really add up and I could only pass off so much on mom's grocery bill before I would get interrogated by Terry as to where all of the random stuff was going.

Karrie's wedding was a blast because I didn't have to sew two dressed together and I actually got to have fun with my friends. Mark helped me with the boys and led everyone to believe that he was a model father and husband. Mark was always so good at fooling people into thinking he was something different than the angry control freak that I had come to know.

Now that the baby was here and Karrie's wedding was past, I lost touch with her. We were just in different times of our lives. I am sure I could call her if I needed her but I never wanted to burden her with my problems. In a way, I alienated myself from my friendships. I knew how most of my friends felt about Mark and it was becoming harder not to get upset with all of the unwarranted advice that was given to me about our relationship. My friendship with Karrie for the next several years would be Christmas and birthday cards in the mail and random calls just to say hello.

I didn't realize at the time how much I would need friends and family to be there for me and the boys. Mark was working out of town more and more and I was struggling to hold everything including my mentality together. After Tony was born, my sister, brother and I had to move mom into a different home that provided more care. One incident in particular made our choice for us. Mom was out walking her dog and got lost trying to get home. We called the police and a helicopter ended up spotting her in the evening when they were doing a traffic report. The helicopter was on the police radio feed and knew to keep an eye out for an older woman walking her dog. Mom got about five miles from home before she was found, we have no idea how many circles she had walked in or how many miles she truly walked that day but we knew we had to never let that happen again.

Of course, during this critical time for my mother, Mark managed to find his way to trouble.

As the years go by I started learning expect some catastrophic bad choice he would make that would end up punishing the kids and I in some way or another. The event that led to another night in jail for Mark was not entirely his fault but he didn't make things better by trying to help himself.

I got the call late in the afternoon from Mark. It was his one call, I wish he would have called his damn parents. I had to call my brother in law, Jack for help bailing Mark out of jail. A few hours earlier, Mark was at a gas station putting gas in his truck on his way home from work when he was surrounded by police. A woman had identified Mark as one of the people who broke into her home and stole her electronics and appliances. Mark was no-where near this home on that afternoon but someone who looked just like him was there to brake in. Steve and one of his friends decided to help themselves to someone else's things. Steve and Mark were mistaken for twins all of the time so it would make sense that the person would have made the mistake. Jack and I got to the jail to get the whole story from Mark but the problem at the time was that Mark was not going to turn his own brother in, so he allowed the police to charge him.

Luckily, the person that helped Steve with the robbery was caught at the pawn shop. Steve was soon to be picked up and a day later and several hundred dollars that we borrowed from Jack and Terry, Mark was released. The woman who thought Mark was Steve realized that she had made a mistake and felt horrible. I was angry at her for putting us through all of that nonsense, but I was also angry at Mark even more. Mark knew his brother was going to hit that house that day and was even thinking of being part of it in some way. All it did was bring more grief to our family.

CHAPTER 6

Sugar and Spice

The move for mom was brutal because we had to take her dog away from her along with most of her possessions. There was no room for decades worth of memorabilia. The memories were sadly gone at this point but Mom knew something wasn't good. We sold the family home to offset the cost of the full-time care that was required at this point. I couldn't take care of the kids and mom without losing my own mind and my third baby. The stress was too much for me to handle my pregnancy during that time. I had a miscarriage and was broken for quite a while. I lost my baby the night before my sister had her fourth child. I didn't handle that very grown up because I couldn't bring myself to get out of bed to go to the hospital and meet my new nephew. Another regret in my list of so many. I went to visit the day they got home, Terry understood because she had suffered from a miscarriage in the past.

Terry decided to stay home from work permanently to raise the kids but ran a daycare to make extra money. This gave me an opportunity to try my hand at school again. I researched cosmetology schools and decided that would be something that I could do that I would like and would eventually get paid to do. My sister volunteered to watch Markie and Tony while I went to school as a favor and a payback for all of the years that I took care of her children. I am still like those kids second mom and have been blessed to be part of their weddings and their kids' lives. I wouldn't be half the person I am today if it weren't for those kids forcing me to get out of bed and be involved in life.

I enrolled in school yet again, this time taking out a loan. All of the money that I wasted of moms was gone and would not be able to fund my new challenge. I really enjoyed going to school because I loved to do hair and nails. The skin part made me a bit grossed out, but I wasn't planning on being an Esthetician. I missed the boys but was only away from them a few hours a day during the week. It was good for them to be around all of the cousins, instead of cooped up in the house with me all of the time. Markie was getting close to preschool age and would need the socialization because I babied him so much. Tony was just what I suspected, a tough little dude. Everything Markie was doing, Tony would do too.

I was having a great time meeting other people and learning all about how to make people feel beautiful. I loved being the Guinee pig when we needed to practice our manicures and pedicures. It was like going to a spa every day. I had to meet a certain number of hours according to the state board tests. After putting in 500 hours each student would test to determine if their skills had progressed enough to work on clients. I tested out with no problem and had many clients that were repeat customers. I also cut hair for everyone in the family for practice. Markie hated sitting in the chair getting his haircut so he kept his a little longer. Tony asked for a haircut once a week to keep it short.

Half-way through my hours, I found out that I was pregnant again. I was having a hard time with all of the chemicals in the building making me sick. My mom also was deteriorating not just her mind was going but her body was starting to give up the fight. I quit school again, just like I had quit on everything else that might have helped me in the future. I was told when I withdrew that the hours I had earned would be saved for five years in the event that I could return. Looking back, I wish I would have had the courage to finish what I had started, fear always preventing me from truly living my life.

Terry and I had to move our mom from the assisted living home we had placed her in to a nursing home. It was like any nursing home I had seen in the movies, absolutely disgusting. We looked at several and chose the best one that was available. Ted was not able to help us with the move because of his own health and living in California. He was recovering from heart surgery and was not able to travel at that time. It felt like a large decision I am sure he would not like, but our hands were tied.

Along with the move for mom, Mark and I had made a move to a bigger home. We were able to sell our first home for twice what it was purchased for because the market was so good. This allowed us to pay off the loan through Terry and mom and buy a fixer upper. Mark was handy and willing to put the work in to make our new larger home livable. The boys still shared a room but we would now have a room for our newest addition. We worked day and night to get the house done before the holidays and the baby were to come. We always made time to visit mom because we didn't know how long we would have her around.

The whole family would load up at one time to go see Mom at the nursing home. We have several pictures of the kids that were around with her so they would remember her, knowing she would never know them. The last time we had a picture of everyone was over Christmas. Terry and I checked mom out of the home for the day so that she could spend the holiday in a comfortable place. We got through Christmas the best that we could with all of the little people running around stressing mom out. She was never happy after dad died and got crankier as time went on, she was not a big fan of anyone including kids. Mark and I took mom back to the home that night and finally put our feet up to rest while the boys played with all of the toys that Santa had brought that morning.

I was not up for shopping the next day for the sales so I let the kids continue to play with all of their new things. That only lasted for a couple of days because they had been given gift cards to the mall. The money was burning a hole in their pockets. All four of us loaded up and went to the mall to catch what was left of the after-Christmas specials. Mark went with the boys to the toy store and I went to Victoria's Secret to get a robe to pack in my bag for the hospital trip that I would be taking in a few weeks to have my little girl. I found the perfect flannel robe, which was odd because I didn't think flannel was a thing for that type of store. I got in line that was out the door and started to have a hot flash. Twenty minutes later I started having contractions and was still in the line. The contractions were so bad someone overheard me breathing heavily and asked if I was in labor. I sure in the hell wasn't waiting in that line for so long and leaving the robe behind. The entire line turned and looked at me and parted for me to pay and get out of there. Just about the time I was at the register, Mark and the kids came walking up. The other customers informed Mark before I had time to speak about my condition.

We quickly left the mall and went home to call Terry and Jack to come take care of the boys. I had a burst of energy so I ran to the grocery store while we waited for the baby sitters to arrive. We got to the hospital about 7pm, Noel was born by 9pm. A perfect red headed baby girl only two weeks early.

Markie and Tony were thrilled to have a doll to play with and show off to all of their cousins. The boys had just started wrestling that season because their cousins were on a team. I had so much support from all of the parents from the team helping me keep track of the boys or taking care of Noel. I was a volunteer team parent and had a lot to do to help out and Mark started to learn the sport to be a volunteer coach. We had so many good friends through those years and I truly enjoyed being part of the organization. I felt like I had purpose because I was helping my kids and meeting people. I am a social person and was kept out of many social activities because Mark didn't like me being out of the house for too long. This was fine with him because he was always there and had an eye on who I was interacting with. Mostly moms and a handful of dad's that didn't seem to threaten Mark's ego.

Not only was I busy with my kids, but was in the middle of yet another move with mom. In the nursing home she had gotten sick. The doctor diagnosed her with E. coli. The suspected reason for catching such a horrible illness was the lack of cleanliness of all of the people who lived there but didn't wash their hands regularly. I never took my kids back when we were moving her because I didn't want to risk them getting infected with anything. We called a priest from the church to give mom her last rights. My brother even flew in to say his goodbyes. That day, all of us kids were standing around mom praying she go quickly to end the suffering. Just as my brother and I were walking out of the door, mom called us by name. Our names, she remembered us for just a brief moment. It wasn't long enough for me to fix our relationship or to apologize for putting her through hell, but it was a moment I will always remember. Once we got approval, we had mom transported to a hospice. The doctor wanted her to be comfortable because she had a living will asking that nothing be done to help her if she got to a point that her body was shutting down. I visited mom the night before the kids had a big wrestling tournament because I knew I wouldn't be able to see her otherwise.

The boys were four and five and weighed the same at this time in their wrestling careers. That would change as the years went by but for now the only people they had to wrestle was each other. They were always rolling around in the house together so this just gave them a bigger space. The first match for them that season was at our home tournament. I was running around like a chicken with its head cut off making sure the referees were being fed or the concession stand hadn't run out of nacho cheese because that would have been a crisis to some people.

I got to the mat just in time to see Markie pin Tony. That was the beginning of the big brother versus little brother competitions. I thought it was all in good fun at first but later on in life it made a huge impact on Tony. If I would have known then what I know now, I might have tried to guide the boys better. As any new parent, we learn by trial and error. I might have had a hand in raising my sister's children but when they went home they were no longer mine to deal with. I was and still am always learning how to parent my kids at every new stage of their lives. I am a work in process.

After the tournament was over and all of the trash had been cleaned and the wrestlers and their families had left for the night, we were able to call it a day and go home. I was so tired but it was a fulfilling exhaustion of being able to provide help for so many people to have a positive experience. I was able to get all three of the kids down at a reasonable time because the boys had school the next day. Just as I fell asleep, the phone rang. It was Terry asking us to come see mom. It was the middle of the night and the kids were sleeping so we called Mark's mom to come to the house. We took Noel with us because she was only six weeks old and was going to need to be fed. We arrived at the hospice to see my poor mother laying their taking sporadic breaths every few minutes. My brother had left the day we moved her to the hospice and she would only end up spending three nights. Terry, Jack, Mark and I didn't speak a word the hours that we watched our mother fade away. Noel started screaming to eat which broke the silence as my mother took her last breath.

Morning light was shining in the room as we all walked out feeling somber but a sense of relief. Mom was done and could be at peace with our father, it is what she had silently wanted for the twelve years they were apart. The next step was to make funeral arrangements and get my brother back on a plane for the service. Terry and I took care of all of the planning and set the funeral for a week out in order to allow any out of town family to attend.

Everyone that had a job took the week off to get things ready for the service. I didn't have a job other than my volunteer commitments for the kids that I still kept because they needed to keep doing things even though the adults in the family stopped functioning. I wasn't thrilled that Mark took the week off because he wouldn't get a pay check. That did not bother him because he knew that we were about to come into a large inheritance.

The funeral was just what our mother would have wanted, a simple Catholic service with the burial to follow. My parents were buried together at Fort Logan National Cemetery for Veterans. My father served in the Army during World War ll and was eligible to be honored with the other vets that had served and lost their lives. My mother's burial was the first time I had been to the cemetery. I am not sure which was more damaging for me, burring my mother or being faced with the grave of my father. I have not and will not go back, it is too painful and I can communicate with my parents through my own thoughts. I know they are watching over me and will always be my guardian angels.

After the dust settled and the families were all back into a routine, the will was read and the inheritance was dispersed. The first order of our business was to pay off our home. As soon as we paid off that home, we started to look for one in Terry's neighborhood. The kids were already all going to the same schools, I just was making the drive every day. They would be able to grow up in the neighborhood all of their friends lived in so it seemed like a smart move.

A month later we were moving into our new home that didn't require any fixing up it was perfect for the kids. The boys still asked to share a room, Noel had her own room and I had a spare bedroom for company. Not that anyone came to visit much, but it was there if we needed the space. Not only did we have a new house, but a new truck, new camper, and Mark had a new dirt bike. He was spending my inheritance faster than I could write the checks.

I managed to finagle a portion into some investments with my mother's financial advisor for future needs. Even though we had put the money from the sale of the previous house into the new house, the funds were dwindling. I am also to blame because I went shopping way too many times for things for the house and the kids. I always got so upset when Mark would spend money that I didn't budget for and in retaliation I would spend money. It was a vicious cycle that would put us back in debt.

Terry and Jack used their inheritance to start a business from the ground up. It was always Jack's dream to own an oil changing store because he loved his cars so much. We all helped with the build in one way or another. I was more of the babysitter and Mark put in some time helping with construction. Their business was soon up and running. Jack quit his construction job to run the business and Terry went back to work now that her kids were old enough to stay home after school.

Ted was the only one of us that actually did something that would help him in his retirement. He invested most of his money and was very good about not spending it on lavish things that weren't needed. At least one of us learned from our parents.

Mark was always coming home and going straight to bed for a nap, then would want dinner and either would be gone with the boys to a practice or hiding in the garage. I never bothered him in the garage because I knew he would just be upset by interruptions. I could hear him hammering and hanging dry wall but didn't care what he was doing as long as he wasn't needing anything from me.

Like any other weekend, we had a wrestling tournament to go to with the boys. This particular weekend was a big deal because it was the Junior State Wrestling Tournament. It was a hard competition for the boys. They no longer were in the same weight class and did not have to wrestle each other unless it was for practice or they were fighting, which was all of the time. Tony did not do so well and was knocked out in the third round not taking a place. Tony was not nearly as thrilled about wrestling as Markie was. Markie worked his way to a second-place finish receiving a plaque with his age and weight engraved on it. He was so excited about the award that he planned to take it to show and tell at school that week.

The next night after dinner we all went to the store to have Markie's name added to the engraving. We took that time to swing by the ice cream shop as an added treat. After we were done with our cones the plaque was ready to be picked up and we could head home for the bedtime routine. Driving up the road we could see huge flames shooting in the sky. As we got closer to our neighborhood we could see the flames were coming from one of the blocks around us. We turned into the entrance and could not believe what we saw next, it was our home.

CHAPTER 7

Burned

Flames shooting high into the sky coming from my home will always be burned in my head. As the car turned the corner, I could not believe my eyes to see my house engulfed in flames. Mark slammed on the breaks and pulled over. Just as he was jumping out, the neighbors swooped in and grabbed all of the kids. I was so thankful because I didn't want them to be as afraid of what was happening as I was. The neighbors took the kids in and gave them hot chocolate and cookies as a diversion. I got out of the truck and my sister ran up and tackled me. The entire neighborhood was on the block watching the house burn. Terry didn't know we were going anywhere that evening so she thought we were in the house and couldn't get out. I started screaming hysterically and was inconsolable for a long time. I kept repeating, "Why? Why? Why?" I was baffled by what was happening and terrified. Once the fire was out and the firemen let us walk through the house I was physically sick to my stomach. Everything was gone, the smell was unbearable, we were covered with ashes and my poor babies only had the clothes on their backs. To this day, I recall exactly what I was wearing because it is all that I had until I got to Terry's to clean up and borrow clothes. I will never be caught dead in red leggings and a flower shirt again.

lost. The firemen started bringing pictures and a couple pieces of antique furniture that I had in the living room out to salvage once they cleared the place for people and pets. We no longer had our two dogs or any other pets at the time. Those pictures and an old chest sent to my Grandmother by my father when he was stationed in Germany during the war was all that we had left.

I walked through the kitchen and could see the sink piled high with the dinner plates from the night before burnt to a crisp. It's funny how people think in times of trauma, I no longer leave dishes in my sink because I was so embarrassed to have the firemen see I had not cleaned up before leaving. I am not sure if that mattered at the time but it sticks in my head and is now one of my quirks. I went to the basement to see the playroom, the other thing that I vividly remember seeing was the Hungry Hippo game the boys had been playing before we left all melted and stuck to the cement floor. It was a reminder of how fortunate I was to have my babies and my life preserved.

Terry and I ran to the store to get a few things while Jack and Mark rented a dumpster and started to clean up the wreckage. I also had scheduled appointments to view apartments as our temporary living arrangements. We did not lose our camper, but that was a last resort to try to have five people living in for any length of time. The insurance company put us in a hotel for a couple of nights until we could get into the apartment that I found to be big enough to fit our family. It was March and summer would be coming so the pool was an added bonus even though we belonged to the swim club by our house. I tried to make this experience as good as I could for the kids.

I also went to the school to pick up Markie and Tony, I knew they would be scared and tired. They had a right to see the house and how precious life can be with or without all of our possessions. I was involved in the PTA and some other groups at the elementary school and was well known. The school had put out a call to every family and asked for donations to help our family in a time of need.

I have never seen anything so amazing. There were trucks full of clothes, toys, food, furniture, you name it. It took days for me to go through everything, not all of the donations were useful to us at the time so I found a battered women's organization to donate what we couldn't use. I did not buy toothpaste for at least a year.

The next step was to find a contractor to rebuild our home. For some reason I was also in charge of picking the right people for the job. I met with two different people and listened to their pitch. Each contractor came to look at the property and assess what it would cost and how the build would be, more importantly how long it would take before we were able to go home. I went with the Italian because I didn't know who to go with and I am Sicilian, it was a gut decision. I was given the plans and had full reign of the cosmetic piece of the house. Initially, we were given a projected finish time of six months.

I had done all I could do for the moment and had busy work running the kids around and setting up our apartment to feel as comfortable as I could. I hated the sight of Mark and how all of this was his fault. About two weeks after the insurance had doled out thousands of dollars helping us get on our feet, we were asked to do an interview with the fire chief and the insurance legal team. Words can't do how I was feeling justice. I was going to have to lie to these people to protect my family and my home. If we were found to be at fault, we would have to pay every penny back and then some.

The kids went to Terry's while we were being interviewed. I didn't need the distractions or the noise in the apartment because I needed to be on my game. Mark and I were automatically on the defense but he didn't seem too bothered by the guilt of the situation. I was sweating bullets trying to act calm about the questioning. After several questions and documenting our statements on a recording, the meeting was over. Now we wait, the final closure of the investigation would take a few more days. In the mean-time, the house was being worked on and I was keeping things as regular as I could.

Days past and finally an official report was delivered to our door. Somehow the investigation was deemed an accidental fire. The second fire made it very hard to prove intentional arson. All in all, it wasn't like Mark was trying to burn the house down. I forgave him the best that I could to get our lives back to some sort of normalcy. The construction continued for months, twelve to be exact. We had only signed a lease for six months based on the assessment from the contractor. Fortunately, we were able to sign a short-term lease for a few more months. During that last few months at the apartment, we decided to get a puppy. If I was going to be potty training Noel, I might as well potty train a dog. The kids were in love with our part wolf, part border collie named Panda. The puppy helped keep the kids busy because they were getting restless being out of the neighborhood missing all of their friends. Unfortunately, we could not stay at the apartment the last month and ended up living in our camper that was parked out in front of our house. If ever I have felt like white trash, that would have been the time. The kids just thought we were on a camping trip but the quarters became very tight and I couldn't wait to get back in the house.

Finally, after a year of waiting in frustration and anticipation, the house was finished. I had recovered from my original anger when we moved back in to everything being brand spanking new. Everyone got to pick their own bedroom sets and decoration for their own rooms. The boys went with bunk beds again. Noel had a little help from me because she wasn't really old enough to decide what she wanted yet. The house looked amazing and was starting to feel like home again.

After all of the money had been paid out for our losses and the construction, we decided to take out a new mortgage on the home to cover things that we wanted to upgrade that wasn't part of the insurance settlement. This was a very foolish move on my part because it would be the beginning of a massive debt for our future. Mark and I were bad with money, we never saved and we spent beyond our means. I convinced Mark that I needed eye surgery because I was tired of wearing glasses and could no longer wear my contacts. There went a few thousand bucks, but I still have good eyesight so I look at is as an investment. If I was to get something, Mark was sure to buy himself something that he had always wanted. Mark went out and bought a motorcycle, without discussing the purchase with me. One day he just rode up and asked if I wanted a ride. More money out the window, not to mention a death trap.

Mark did not get to ride the bike for long before he found himself in trouble. One of his friends was getting married and there was a bachelor party downtown that Mark attended. He did not take his bike that night, he drove my car. The kids and I watched movies and ate popcorn, then turned in like many other nights. I was asleep on the couch when Mark came barreling through the door at 3am. Mark was a big fan of guns and had a couple of shot guns for hunting and a hand gun locked in a gun cabinet in our room. He stormed upstairs, opened the cabinet and loaded the gun. When he came downstairs I was screaming at him in question. Mark had been followed home from the bar that night and was planning on protecting himself. He ran outside swinging the gun around like it was a toy. The car pulled up. I was already on the phone with the police because I was afraid for the kids and I. I am not sure what was more terrifying, Mark or the dark car out front.

The police were already on their way, which I thought was strange because I was still on the phone with dispatch when they pulled up. The driver of the car had called them reporting a drunk driver swerving all over the road. Once again, Mark was hauled away in handcuffs. This time in front of the kids and neighbors. I was shaking like a leaf mostly because of the gun. One of the officers brought the weapon into the house and helped me lock it up securely to keep it out of harm's way. I was able to go bail Mark out the next morning. I didn't want to but it seemed like the thing to do. Mark was furious at me for calling the cops. I explained that I was trying to protect our family but in the end, he blamed me for the arrest. Mark blamed me for anything and everything all of the time, I was used to it.

Another DUI with more jail time for Mark. He was allowed to do a work release program in order to make money for the family. This time he was in for thirty nights and all day on weekends. I wasn't thrilled to explain his absence to all of the people involved in the kids' sporting events especially because he was a coach. Then again, I was really getting a bad taste in my mouth for him and his ability to act like he was a model citizen to everyone but me.

More money out of the account to cover the court and legal fees. Mark insisted on hiring an attorney because he didn't feel he was at fault. The thirty-day sentence along with fines was the best the attorney could do considering Mark's previous driving record. I think that hardest part of Mark being in jail was how it would impact the kids. We lived in an upscale neighborhood and there were many character judges willing to point out how inappropriate the situation appeared. I was still trying to maintain the perfect family to the kids, our families and friends. Mark wasn't making the job easy and I found that I had become quite an actress always standing by my man.

Just after Mark finished his jail time, I had to have my wisdom teeth pulled. My teeth were killing me and something had to be done. I needed to have them out when I was in high school but since I was in charge of my own life, I decided to forego that procedure out of fear of pain. It was time, I explained to the dentist that I was very afraid and wanted to be asleep during the minor surgery. I dropped the kids off to school and Noel off with Elizabeth. Mark took the day off of work to take me because I was not able to drive myself after the extraction. We walked in, sat in the waiting room filling out paperwork for a while before I was called back. The nurse specifically looked at Mark and asked that he wait while the procedure was going on until I was awake and could be taken home.

As usual, I had a feeling of fear but wanted the pain to go away. I went back and got hooked up to the IV. I was asked to count backwards from twenty and reassured that I would be done before I knew it. I came to being rushed on a gurney down the hospital corridor with Mark on one side and my sister hysterical on the other. I had a reaction to the anesthesia and my heart stopped with only one tooth being pulled. The dentist called for an ambulance and tried to reverse the medication immediately. Mark was nowhere to be found when I was being loaded into the ambulance. He explained to the dentist when asked why he didn't stay as requested that he was very nervous for me and needed to go outside to relax. Draw your own conclusions, he always needed to relax and was never around when you needed him. He pulled up just as the ambulance was driving away, the dentist told him to follow me to the hospital because I would need him.

I ended up in the cardio unit with a bunch of old people having my heart tested. The doctors were baffled by a girl in her early twenties having heart issues over a simple dental surgery. Once again feeling betrayed by Mark but concerned with the big picture put my feelings to the side. Over the years I had been hiding my feelings so well it was like nothing to me. Eventually feelings that are hidden come out and it's not pretty. I was in the hospital for two days having tests run to make sure I wasn't suffering from heart issues. It runs in my family and has affected my brother from a very early age so all precautions were necessary to rule out disease. I was finally given a good bill of health with the warning to let medical staff know of my allergic reaction if any future surgeries were needed. The dentist booked an operating room in the hospital to have the remaining teeth removed just in case there was another reaction.

I was back in the hospital a week later getting the teeth pulled. Another reaction but this time with the surgical staff in the room I was treated on the spot. All of the teeth were out and I got to spend another night in the hospital as a precaution. I didn't mind, it gave me a little break from home.

Once I was back at home and fully recovered from my heart scare and chipmunk cheeks it was back to the old grind. I was the taxi for the kids along with the maid and chef. This is the life I had chosen and was doing the best I could to make it work. Mark suggested that we take a vacation with what little we had left of the savings from the mortgage loan. I had already cashed in a bunch of the investments from my inheritance to cover the legal and hospital bills. I was ready to get out of Denver for a break, so we did what anyone with a handful of kids would do, we went to Disney World.

The trip was fantastic, the kids met all of their favorite Disney characters and rode every ride at least twice. We played the ultimate tourists and hit all of the places on the recommended list of activities. I always feel truly at home by the ocean so I was in heaven. Mark and I were getting along again, I can't help but wonder if it is because we weren't home dealing with the everyday bullshit. Somehow, he managed to smuggle drugs on the plane so as not to be without them on such a long family vacation. I hated that he was always disappearing on the kids and I but I became immune to his behavior because it was more important to me that the kids never found out what type of person their dad truly is. Mark had always been what I would consider to be a "Disney Land Dad", he just liked to do fun things with the kids and not deal with discipline issues or school conferences.

I was getting worn out chasing the kids around and chalked it up to not sleeping well in the hotel. I put on my big girl pants and continued to do the tourist thing complete with sunscreen on our noses and a camera hanging from my neck. The weeklong trip started to become long about day 5 when the kids were getting tired of going and going. We never have taken a vacation that we don't have the whole day and half the night planned to wear them out. I was ready to come home even though I knew it would be the last vacation we took for a while.

I was very sick on the plane and had hoped the kids would not get the stomach flu too. The flu was kicking my ass at this point and I stayed in bed for a couple of days accept to take care of the kids. I dragged myself up and out of the house to get the kids to school and went to the doctor, I was a mess. I explained my symptoms but wasn't really listening to myself speak because if I would have thought it through, I would have known what was wrong. Baby number four coming next spring. Hell of a vacation that summer.

CHAPTER 8

New Beginnings

The last pregnancy was the hardest, I was sick with something from the time I found out until I literally gave birth. I am sure it was due partially because I was getting older compared to when I had Markie and because I still maintained my volunteering at the school and with the sporting teams the kids were all involved in. I even had Noel enrolled in a little gymnastics and dance school along with soccer. The boys played baseball, football and wrestled along with swimming lessons. I encouraged the kids to try as many things as they could to find out what they liked best. The clarinet and saxophone were on the list for the boys along with all of the athletics. I am not going to lie, I am a sports fan and loved to watch the kids excel at their various positions or weight classes. The band thing was a challenge to buy into. The band teacher at the school had a final performance set for Markie as a graded performance. The date of the recital conflicted with the little league baseball play-off game, I went to the teacher and explained the conflict. The band nerd said he would fail Markie if he was not in attendance for the concert. Markie and I had a mom to kid conversation and picked baseball. It would be the one and only F as a grade for Markie throughout the rest of his academic career. I basically told the teacher to stick the clarinet where ever he sees fit. Tony gave up on learning the sax about two weeks into practices, it was interfering in his play time.

I might have been a little grouchy because it was spring time and I was as big as a house and constantly in and out of the doctor office trying to stay as healthy as I could before the baby came. I will always be superstitious because of my dad getting in his accident on a Friday the 13th so I was trying very hard to not have a baby on that day in March. On the twelfth I was hosting a wrestling banquet and was very busy running around making sure it was the event of the year. Everything went great and I was feeling good. The next morning, I woke up to get ready to run errands and low and behold my water broke. It was early on the thirteenth but I wasn't having contractions so I was sure I could close my legs until at least midnight. By four in the afternoon I was begging to be done with the pregnancy. My beautiful little girl Morgan was born. I know she hates the way we celebrate her birthday but she goes along with it because it's all she knows. We celebrate her day on the twelfth or the fourteenth every year.

The first two weeks of Morgan's life were picture perfect. The other kids were thrilled to show her off and she was a perfect little angel. Third week of life took a turn in the wrong direction. Morgan woke up one night and cried out of control for hours. I did everything, changed her, fed her, rocked her, nothing was helping this baby, I was getting scared that something was terribly wrong. Unlike the other kids, she was hardly early and had plenty of time to bake in my belly. Mark and I took her to the doctor as soon as we got the other kids off to school. The pediatrician wanted us to meet him at the hospital to run tests to rule out meningitis. What a horrible thing to watch your baby have a giant needle go into her tiny little spine while being told not to let her move or it could cause permanent damage. I am not good under pressure so it took both Mark and I to hold her still.

We waited many hours to find out if Morgan was seriously ill. The doctor came in and discussed the side effects of having colic. He explained that something was making her stomach hurt so bad she couldn't eat. I tried many different formulas instead of breast feeding, she was eating but was always spitting up. My tiny little infant had to be put on baby doses of antacid medication to help the pain. It didn't stop her from crying or feeling pain all of the time. Morgan cried from six in the morning until midnight every day for the next two years.

I was losing it because I was having to take care of her and all of the other kids and their activities. God forbid they get sick because I was struggling just to take care of the baby. Somehow, we managed and got used to her crying. There were many times I would load up the four kids to go to the store and be stared at because of the constant whaling from the baby. I just ignored all of the dirty looks and under breath comments, no one had walked a mile in my shoes and I dare anyone to approach a mom with bags the size of luggage under her eyes with a screaming child in hand. We managed, people would hold the baby when I needed to be watching the other kids wrestle or do a floor routine. There is also a little thing called a cry room at church, we had it all to ourselves because of all of the nose. A side note to the cry room, when Morgan stopped crying all of the time, the boys still asked to sit in the cry room because they wanted to play Legos instead of listen about God. I laughed internally and made them sit at the front of the church after that request.

Terry and Jack were doing well with their business and decided they needed to buy a bigger house in the neighborhood. I am not sure why I thought this was a good idea, but they offered to sell us the house they were currently in because we could fix up the basement and the kids could have their own rooms. Mark and I discussed moving again we already had our home exactly how we wanted it after the fire. I thought about it for a long time and we decided to make the move again. A few weeks later, we were moving my sister's stuff out of our new home and into their new home. The house was much larger than the one we were in and allowed everyone to have their own space. Our backyard fence had a gate to Terry's front yard, good fences make good neighbors. When we wanted to see my family, we could and vice versa.

Mark spent the next several months reforming the basement to be the perfect area for the boys to live. Each would have their own room with a large front room and a walk out door. I knew the walk out door would be a mistake but it was according to fire code to have an exit and I was not about to revisit and fire codes. The basement was done before the boys decided to use the door without letting us know, it was just a matter of time. I painted each of the kid's rooms specifically to the things they liked. Markie had a checkered flag painted on one wall in his team colors and the team mascot painted on the other wall. Tony had flames coming up from the ground, not sure if it was the memory of the fire or if he was just truly devilish. Noel loved monkeys and requested a jungle theme on her wall. Morgan had taken an interest in turtles and would eventually have an ocean scene painted on her wall. I loved arts and crafts so this was right up my alley.

The family was so busy, I had to start a calendar that was color coded to keep everything in order. Mark and I were getting along as good as always, which was him being in control of everything that mattered to him. He realized that the last several months had been tedious and suggested we take the honeymoon that we never had after the wedding. I was enticed with talks of the sun and the beach with no diapers, bottles or uniforms to wash.

The Caribbean was the front-runner on the list of places to visit. I had never been and it was much cheaper because it was the hot season so not as many tourists. I like the heat and planned on being in the ocean or the pool. A month later our bags were packed, I had divvied up the kids to go between family and friends for the four nights we would be gone.

Traveling with just Mark was like a blast from the past and our Mexico trip. I asked if he was doing anything illegal that I should know about before we boarded the plane. I was never told the truth. It was Mark's way of not making me an accomplice or listening to me nag. As we were landing, the pilot came on the speaker and warned us not to use the bathrooms in the airports and to get right on the bus to our various hotels. I wasn't sure what I had gotten myself into but I knew it couldn't be good. The first thing I had to do was go to the bathroom when we got off of the plane. I told Mark that I was going and to wait outside for me to make sure nothing happens. After four kids, a person just doesn't wait to go to the bathroom. I got in shut the stall door, no sooner did I sit down and a Jamaican woman popped her head over the top of the stall. Standing on the adjacent toilet looking right at me. I was in the right position because I would have pissed my pants otherwise. The woman was offering to sell me drugs. A lightbulb went off and I figured out why this place was on Mark's radar. I quickly finished my business, said "No" about a hundred times and got out of there as fast as possible.

I told Mark what had just happened and he assured me it was an isolated incident and to relax, we were on vacation. Not so isolated, the bus driver and the hotel clerk offered us a pleather of drugs at a low cost. We were warned by our bus boy to stay in the compound and we would be safe. If we went out in the town we would be targets as Mark was so fair skinned he was referred to as a redneck. That wasn't a big stretch, people called him that at home based on his country upbringing. It was late at night when we arrived so we just walked around the property to familiarize ourselves with the lay of the land.

The next day we woke up and headed straight to the beach. Much more my speed, there were boats and snorkeling trips to take during the day. Fancy dinners and music at night, it was really paradise if we stayed within the walls. On each end of the property were walls built to keep us in with armed guards on each side for our protection from the locals. The sight was very disturbing but I tried to maintain my vacation mentality and make the best of the trip.

After the first two days and nights spent within the walls of the resort, Mark got bored. The first problem was the hotel staff pointing out that we should not go out of the property limits, being told not to do something only fueled Mark. After breakfast we walked out of the door and into the streets of a small quaint beach town.

A foot out of the building and we were already approached. The scam was for us to rent a dirt bike to take a guided tour of the country. The first stop was a little bistro on top of a hill by a movie set. It was gorgeous and so far, we were having a fantastic excursion. The next stop was Bob Marley's garden, both of them. The garden I loved had a park bench surrounded by colorful tropical flowers and plants. It was so peaceful I could have spent the rest of the afternoon in that spot. The other garden was a crop of marijuana plants taller than me, which is not saying much but it still seemed extreme. I was disgusted, but that didn't seem to bother Mark.

As the day went on, we explored more of countryside. The poverty was so hard to see and reminded me yet again of how blessed I am. We were lead to a little village with a school and a church directly surrounded by houses that looked like I wouldn't camp there if given the option. A girl came up to us in a plaid school uniform dress that made me think back to my elementary school days. The little girl was absolutely charming, she asked that we take a picture with her for our vacation album. I thought that would be a nice addition to the album compared to the ridiculous pot plant picture we had to take. Once the picture was taken the little girl held out her hand for money. I was surprised that this child was part of the scheme. I refused to give her anything claiming I had nothing on me and have my own children to take care of, but wished her luck. The tour guide showing us around happened to be the girl's Uncle. He was less than pleased with my lack of money and threatened to leave us out there in the middle of nowhere with no way back. I was scared to death, we gave them all the cash we had on us at the time. We followed the tour guide back in fear that there was going to be another trick up his sleeve. It was dark when we got back to our hotel, I had never been so happy to be in the confines of the walls. Once again, I was furious with the selfish nature of Mark to have put us both in such danger. I called my kids one by one and told them how much I loved them and missed them.

The flight home was scheduled to land in Miami for customs check before getting us back to Denver. Everyone got off of the plane to go through the process of coming back into the States. I was ready to be home and just wanted to catch our connecting flight, but we had a two-hour layover. All of the people on the plane filed out one by one into the customs area. There were dogs in the corridor sitting there waiting for the next idiot to get caught with drugs. The passengers were lined up against a wall waiting to see what was going to happen. A dog came and sat in between me and one other passenger. I would never think of doing drugs and certainly wouldn't travel with them on me, but I know who would. At that moment I started thinking about how I was going to deal with the next mess. It turned out the person to the left of me had the drugs in her purse. These dogs were trained to find cocaine, luckily Mark was only carrying marijuana, different dogs search for other drugs and those dogs were not at that gate. Once we were cleared to catch our next flight, I went outside and started sobbing. I was so tired of dealing with Mark and his drugs, it was wearing me down but there was no escaping my life, crying was all I could do at that moment. Mark found the situation to be humorous and had the nerve to take a picture of me standing in the center of the walkway crying.

Our flight landed later that evening and I insisted on retrieving all of the kids that night, I didn't want to wait another moment to lay eyes on them. They were all happy we were home, almost as happy as all of the people that hosted them while we were gone. Life would get back to normal for everyone.

I jumped into my routine the next day by running the kids to their games and playdates. I didn't bother to argue with Mark over how upset and angry I was about the danger he put me in more than once on vacation. Mark always said I was making things up in my head and that he didn't do anything wrong. He knew no one would believe me, he always led people to believe that I was crazy or losing my mind the way Mom did a few years back.

The summer was coming to an end, the kids and I had to get our pool time in as much as possible before school started and our leisure afternoons were replaced with homework and practices. I bought each of the kids a new suit for the pool because everything was on clearance to make room for fall clothes and school supplies. One of the last days at the pool was a doozy for my family. I had rounded up Terry's kids and my kids to do a lunch and swimming. I had my girls out of the water and in the shower getting cleaned up for their dance class. All of the other kids were still playing in the pool but didn't need my supervision due to all of the swimming lessons, along with the lifeguards on duty, I didn't even bat an eye not watching them for a few minutes.

The girls were sitting on a lounge chair waiting patiently to have their hair braided for class. In the background I heard someone scream, "Oh my God, he fell!" I turned to check on all of the kids playing in the deep end on the diving boards, a quick glance and turned back to Noel's hair. I was sure all of the kids I had were safe because I didn't recognize the suit of the person who fell. The entire summer I had been looking at the same kids in the same suits. One of the other parents came running up to me telling me to get to Tony. I turned to look and saw the lifeguard trying to stop the bleeding, I got across the pool deck as fast I as I could to witness one of my babies laying there lifeless covered in blood. Tony was getting ready to do a swan dive off of the high dive, the board was wet and Tony slipped but not close to the water, he hit the cement from a twelve-foot drop. The lifeguard was doing everything he had been trained to do as the sirens got closer and closer to get Tony to the hospital. The other kids were in the pool and had seen the fall. They were terrified as was I. A couple of the other parents that I had known for years volunteered to take the rest of the kids to Terry's house as Tony was loaded into the ambulance. I jumped in hysterical because he wouldn't wake up. The paramedics got the bleeding to stop and Tony opened his eyes. He was out of it and didn't know what was going on but could hear the sirens thinking it was awesome that he got a ride in an ambulance.

The doctors had been called ahead of time and were ready to treat Tony. I was still in a wet swimming suit and was freezing. Partially because I was scared and in shock. The nurses were kind enough to give me some scrubs to wear to warm up. I can't get rid of them still because they are comfortable and because they are a visual reminder of the day I almost lost my boy. Tony ended up with nine staples on the inside of his head and fifty stitches on the outside of his head. He had partial memory loss and struggled for a few weeks after the accident. School was starting in a week but I kept him home for the first two weeks to recover. He would miss football that season because of the head injury. Once he got back into school, I would get a call an hour or two after the start of class to come pick him up because of headaches. I went diligently to pick him up when I was called, until I started to realize Tony had figured out how to manipulate the teacher into good grades with little or no effort because of his injury. Once I started to catch on, I took Tony to our pediatrician for a checkup. Tony had recovered, I am not sure when but the teacher along with the family had been played for a while. All I could say was how thankful I was that he is still here and how fortunate Tony is to have nine lives.

CHAPTER 9

Boys Will Be Boys

O nce Tony was ready to resume activities, we were able to get back to what we all knew and loved. Wrestling season was just beginning, I was apprehensive of how hard it might be on Tony's head injury from the summer but we let him wrestle anyway. The boys had countless injuries over the years, some serious, some not so serious. They were boys and didn't hold back because they were afraid, they had no fear. I am sure they get that from their father because I was always afraid of something. It takes a great effort for me to not run onto the mat or the field when one of the kids goes down. My girls were growing up the same, they all played to their best ability full steam ahead. I used to be like that, I don't know what happened other than I became a parent and realized that I am not invincible.

Wrestling was getting expensive because Markie was already planning on getting a scholarship for college. He wasn't even in high school but was already setting goals. Tony liked to wrestle but not to the extent that Markie did, so when it came time to send them to camps or get extra coaching we would have to decide if Tony would really benefit or if the money would be spent better elsewhere on him. We hired a private coach for Markie who made it to the Olympics when he was younger. Markie was coming along great but between his private coach and the twenty hours a week in gymnastics that Noel was putting in, the funds got very low. It was time for me to pick up some kind of work from home gig that would help offset all of the sports fees.

I still had Morgan at home, I needed to have something that would allow me to take care of the kids and make money. I started doing some odd jobs, at one time I had a job as a bookkeeper for Terry and Jack's auto store. I also was an assistant to one of Markie's best friend's dad in the mortgage business. I was able to work from home for both of those jobs, they did not cut the funding problems I was having so I started selling Herbalife. That was fine for a while, but I am not much of a salesperson. I have never cared what people bought so the vitamin business was short lived. I worked for the store and the mortgage company for about a year making a few bucks here and there. It was hard to work for family as I had already learned doing daycare for so many years.

Wrestling season was winding down and the kids were already practicing baseball. Noel still chugging away every day at the gym for dance and gymnastics and Morgan not old enough or interested enough in anything to participate yet. Morgan would be starting school after the summer was over but she was more of a Mommy's girl and wanted to be wherever I was at the time. One of the first baseball tournaments that we had for Markie was in Fort Collins. The kids all loved when his sports took us out of town because we either stayed in hotels or camped out. These trips were like mini vacations to our family. We all would attend the games and then go swimming or out to eat which was a treat for a family of six. The second night of the tournament, the kids gathered to go swimming and the parents all sat by the pool having cocktails and socializing. I always enjoyed these times because it gave me an opportunity to be around people other than Mark. I made a great friend in one of the moms that was just as miserable in her marriage as I was, we had plenty to commiserate about with each other. I didn't get much grief from Mark about being friends with Jamie because he was friends with her husband John, who coincidentally was my boss with the mortgage business. Our families traveled together and got together once a week for dinner after church or baseball. It was almost as if we were a normal functioning family during those years. The kids all got along so well and grew up to be friends for life.

The night we were all by the pool, Mark excused himself from the other parents. I knew what he was going to do but didn't draw attention because of the shame I always felt when he left to get high. It was never going to get any better because he had no intention of stopping, but would still try to avoid the kids finding out. After about an hour, I started to wonder what the hell was taking him so long. Everyone started to ask where he was and I of course said he must have turned in for the night. I gathered up the kids and got them to the hotel to get ready for bed. Mark and the car were both gone, I assumed he went to a bar and went to bed myself. The hotel phone rang, which is always disturbing because they are so loud and we don't get calls on vacation usually. I picked up quickly to not wake the four kids that I had just gotten to settle down. Mark was on the other end and explained that he had been picked up by the police and needed to be bailed out. The car had been impounded so I had no way of getting to the bank and to the jail in a town of which I knew nothing about. I was forced to go knock on John and Jamie's door and ask for help. The jig was up, I had to explain that Mark got caught getting high in the car out in the parking lot of the hotel. He had the keys in the ignition listening to the radio while he sat there when a police officer driving through the lot spotted him. Given the time of night, the officer decided to check out if the man in his car was supposed to be there or not. Mark was arrested for another DUI, his third offence. John drove me to the bank to withdraw money and then went with me to pick up Mark. The only reason Mark was able to get out on bail was because we weren't from that town. The police department allowed his case to be sent to our county for convenience of Mark and jail. It was a small town and was over flowing with violators, the police were more than happy to release Mark to our county. This meant we got to pay fines to one county for the actual offence and fines to another for his incarceration time.

Here we go again, court appearances, jail time, and dollar after dollar wasted on Mark's bad choices. Mark was being held after being sentenced to sixty days in our county jail. No need to visit him, he was stuck in the holding jail for a solid week before a bed opened up in the work release program. The judge gave him the option to do the release program to provide for our family. This was the same program he had been in a few years back, he was quite used to the process. So, used to the process that he was able to act as if he was taking the bus because his license had been revoked but really drove his car and parked a couple blocks from the jail. The bus stop was also a little way from the jail, every morning those inmates that were scheduled to take the bus were let out and expected to check back in after their work day. If a person were using the bus as transportation they would be allotted and hour at the beginning and the end of the day for travel. Mark would walk towards the bus stop, get in his car, go to work and then come home to take the boys to practices. I was on edge for two months, if he would have been caught driving or avoiding his jail time it would have meant prison time. Our family would not have any income if that happened. Mark never saw things rationally, I was told I was being dramatic. There was a part of me that wanted to make an anonymous phone call but the other part needed the money for the mortgage.

Speaking of mortgage, I encouraged Mark into taking out a second on our home to pay down debt from credit cards and legal fines. Our debt was growing and growing but I was not going to let the kids suffer and miss out on anything because of their father's mistakes. I was able to do the mortgage stuff without paying added fees because of my job with John. It almost made going into debt too easy.

One Saturday during baseball season, Jamie and I with another mom were driving the boys to baseball. John was working and Saturday was the one-day Mark was stuck in jail. I was too busy with the kids to go by and would see him the next week considering he was always breaking the law to come to the house. Jamie offered the other mother the chance to work at the school that she worked at a part time position. The other mother immediately declined because she was getting ready to retire and did not want to put that on hold. Jamie turned and asked if I would like to interview for the job. I accepted thinking this could help our family debt. I didn't consult Mark before I made the appointment for the interview. When I did have a chance to talk to him, he was not happy about me working and not being available at all times. I had to explain that it was only for a few hours a day and would not interfere in my chores or taking care of the kids. The bottom line was that we needed the money and I was going to do the best I could to help. I always took care of the finances so I was the one who saw what kind of trouble we were in, it wasn't pretty. Mark didn't know how to take care of the bills or write a check but he sure mastered taking money out of an ATM.

I met with the Principal and the Financial Secretary the following week at the school. The interview lasted about fifteen minutes before I was offered the job. I would be assisting the Financial Secretary who had the accounting job for the school. This job was something I was confident I could do with my bookkeeping background. The timing was perfect because my sister was selling her business in a few weeks. They weren't able to run it the way it needed to be run and found they had better get out of being owners before they lost all of the money invested. I would start when school started which gave me time to help Terry close shop before starting my new job. Mark was surprised that I was able to get a job, he always let me know what I was good for and working wasn't one of them. Mark was very hard on my self-confidence, it took him years to break me down and is taking years for me to build myself back up.

I started my job toward the end of July to get training classes complete in order to be ready for the beginning of the school year. Mark was released about the same time and got a wild hair to go to Sturgis, South Dakota for the annual motorcycle rally. I told him not to go, we didn't have the money and he didn't have a valid license for another year at least. Mark didn't care, he told me he was going with or without me. I decided I had better go to make sure he didn't get into trouble again.

We took off Friday right after work with nothing but our tent and an extra pair of jeans. I had never been to a motorcycle rally and was nervous about riding that long on the back of the bike. Mark loved that bike and I was so mad at him for getting it without discussing it with me. I decided to go get a big tattoo in the middle of my back to irritate him for having the bike. I went with my sister in law and didn't let Mark know until my tramp stamp was permanently in place. Mark was angry, but that was the reaction I was looking for out of him. Sometimes I would grow a pair and stand up to him, most times I would cower. My tattoo was four red roses intertwined in leaves to represent each one of the kids. I have one other tattoo on my ankle that I got to represent Mark and I, it is two roses in the shape of a heart. Mark only had one little tattoo on his arm that he got when he turned eighteen, but it seemed like enough to fit in with the rest of the bikers.

Sturgis was like another world with all of the nudity and drinking being done out in public. We camped out for two nights and went to the concerts. If you like people watching that is a good place to go. That trip was very quick and Mark managed to get through without doing any damage to either of us. It was over just as fast as it began, which was fine with me.

School was starting and I was well into my job before the students showed up. My boys were going into junior high, Noel was at the grade school and Morgan in preschool. Everyone was busy and I was starting to spread my wings. Mark was distant towards me but I was so busy I didn't have time to notice his attitude. Things changed as soon as I got my first paycheck, Mark decided the job was a good thing. This gave him the idea that he could withdraw money whenever he wanted not taking into consideration all of the bills we had to pay. The more money you make, the more you spend. We never saved anything and just kept spending. The only savings we would have was his retirement pension that was automatically deducted before he could get his hands on it.

I was hired full time and was hardly home until the last minute when I needed to have dinner on the table. I was spreading myself thin and it was taking its toll on me. I started to go to church more with the kids, because of all of the sports we had drifted out of the routine of going. My sister n law and I were both raised Catholic and had found out that we were going against the rules of the church by receiving communion because our marriages were not blessed in the church. We convinced Mark and Steve to go through the marriage prep classes at our church so we could have a double ceremony. That was theoretically the third time I made the mistake of marrying Mark if you count our pretend wedding at prom. Part of my reasoning beside going along with what the church wanted was to try to make my own marriage to Mark more fulfilling, I wanted so badly to live happily ever after. Life didn't change much after the vows were exchanged. The kids had school the day after our celebration and it was back to the basics of life.

Markie was excelling at school and sports as usual and Tony was struggling as usual. Tony never liked school. I learned this early on when I dropped the boys off to preschool one day and got a call five minutes after I had been home to find out Tony ran away. We had walked to and from school enough that he figured out how to escape during recess and headed home. From that day on I would fight him to stay in school. Tony also was not as active as Markie and started to put on some weight. In junior high the kids can be cruel to each other, if you aren't the stereo type person that a thirteen-year-old girl liked then you would get made fun of. I don't think that applies only to our neighborhood junior high, I believe it is all schools full of people going through puberty. Tony was girl crazy but the girls were mean to him for being overweight. The ridiculing just made Tony a mean resentful boy. He and Markie were always competing with each other. It was as if Tony couldn't do the things Markie was doing any more so he went in the opposite direction to seek acceptance and became the tough guy that everyone was afraid of getting hit by. Tony was a bully because he didn't know how to get attention in a positive way anymore.

I got very tired of downplaying Markie's accomplishments to avoid upsetting Tony. I stopped babying Tony and just let him deal with the consequences, it was a lesson for him to understand that people who do good things and try hard get rewarded, he wasn't understanding the lesson what so ever. Tony started to get into more and more trouble at school and was suspended a few times during his seventh and eighth grade years. Towards the end of junior high, he figured out getting sent home to be with me was worse than suffering through school. He was friends with the same kids from grade school and they were all misbehaved, this made things so much harder on everyone when the pack of them were up to no good.

Tony was a very depressed boy because of the teasing he was receiving from the other kids at school. He had a couple of really good friends that he hung out with but they were teased as well. I would not find out until a few years later but this was the beginning of a very bad drug addiction. Tony's friends got into pain killers, a gate way too much worse. I still don't know who actually gave the boys these painkillers and if I ever find out they had better be prepared for a battle. Like all addicts, there was a need for more or stronger. I didn't see the changes in Tony because he had been hard to deal with for a long time.

My other kids were always so willing to help out and respectful at that time, all I could think is that Tony was just mad about everything and treated everyone poorly. I didn't see how truly unhappy he was or how he was dealing with his feelings. By the time Tony was a freshman he was completely absorbed in the drug scene. I still didn't see it or maybe I just wasn't wanting to see it because other people were starting to ask questions that I was in denial about.

Markie had already lettered in his freshman year of wrestling and was voted team captain. He went to state that season which was huge because of his age. Tony also lettered his freshman year and I was thankful the wrestling team kept him eligible because football wasn't as successful. The boys were growing up fast and the door to the basement was used more than our front door either sneaking people in or out of the house. I tried to stay on top of all of the kids but the girls were starting to do much more and I was running around taking care of them.

Focusing on the girls gave me the chance to make sure they were busy and behaved. Noel was always around older girls because she was an exceptional athlete and was advanced in gymnastics and softball. The downside of her competing with older girls was her attitude. She had started to act and talk like a teenager before her time. The attitude lasted a few years and Noel became more and more disrespectful towards me but her father could do no wrong. I still had my little Morgan who was so sweet and loved school, it was a blessing because I was about ready to give up on the math homework that I was helping Noel with. Much like Tony, Noel wasn't a big fan of school and struggled with her grades.

My life got much less stressful when Markie started to drive. At lease he could drive himself and Tony to school and practices. We got him a car for his fifteenth birthday so that he could learn how to drive that year on his permit in his own vehicle. After he got his license a classmate of his got into a horrible accident and died. The accident supposedly could have been prevented or not fatal if the girl had been driving a bigger car. The next day Mark told Markie he needed to drive our truck and Mark would drive the little compact car we had purchased. I was not willing to sacrifice my son's life because the car was too small.

Tony was angry that he didn't get a car for his fifteenth birthday like Markie did the year before. It is not that we were playing favorites, it's more that Tony was not making good choices and didn't deserve the reward. I was reluctant to let him get his driver's license because he was so careless. I was hoping he would straighten up if we put him through driver's education to get his permit. I refused to teach any of the kids to drive after I took Markie for a spin. I feared for my life with all of them behind the wheel. After all, I changed all of the diapers and potty trained them, Mark could teach them to drive.

Tony went through all of his Driver's Ed classes and got his license. The year of his sixteenth birthday we took him to a junk yard and got him a slightly abused first car. Now I had both boys driving, talk about nerve racking. Tony was still wrestling but had completely quit the football team. I was happy he was still focusing on something positive. Tony was losing weigh but I chalked it up to all of the training that was involved with the team. I was wrong but once again just couldn't bring myself to think the he would do drugs.

As if life wasn't crazy enough with the four kids running in different directions and both parents working full time to get by pay check to pay check, our dog Panda got sick. I took her to the vet to find she had cancer that was not curable. Mark and I decided to have her put to sleep to end her suffering. All of the kids were mad and so upset about her dying, it took them days to start talking to us again. Shortly after we lost Panda, we adopted Chester our black pug. Neither Mark or I was looking for another dog, this one just fell into our lives. Noel's good friend from the gymnastics team had been given this puppy as a gift from her mother. It turned out they could not take care of the dog where they were moving to and asked if we would take him. Chester was adorable and needed a home and we were happy to have a dog back in the house.

Life started to get into a routine for all of us and was tolerable for me. Markie was doing great, I was ignoring Tony's drug addiction and Mark's for that matter. The girls were busy with sports and I was on summer vacation. I loved my six weeks a summer off from work and used every bit of it to do anything other than work. Markie and Tony had a part time job as the field crew at the local sports arena. I was happy they were making a few extra bucks instead of bleeding me dry all summer.

Saturday mornings were busy for the boys because of the track meets they had to set up for and the girls always had gymnastics or softball. I was up braiding Noel and Morgan's hair for the meet they had that morning. The phone rang just as my hands were tied up with hair, Noel answered the phone and stated our friend Greg needed to talk to me about Tony. I thought the call was odd because they didn't have wrestling but I promptly got on the line to find out Tony had been placed under arrest for being under the influence of alcohol. Tony was out the night before with his friends and stayed the night at one of their homes. He managed to get himself put together enough to try to make it to work but was followed in to the arena by the police, he was swerving all over the road at 6am and was completely wasted. Greg was our friend so instead of following the letter of the law and cuffing Tony and hauling his ass to detox, he asked that Mark and I come pick him and the vehicle up. I knew from the moment we picked Tony up that he would not understand what it is to pay consequences for making a bad decision if the cops were treating him special.

I was furious with Tony but having been married to a heavy drinker, I knew my ranting would fall on deaf ears as long as he was still hammered. I waited for the hangover to kick in before I laid into him about my level of disappointment. I didn't have to threaten to take the car away, the license was pulled by the police and I had the keys. I attempted to ground him but that damn basement door was going to be his way out if he wanted to leave. I couldn't look at him for days because I was so upset at what he had done.

Tony was sentenced to community service and fines. He was a minor and did not have to spend any time in jail but had to complete alcohol evaluation classes that cost money along with random breathalyzer tests requested by the probation officer. Tony only attended a handful of classes even though he could carpool with his father who also was court ordered to attend classes, Tony didn't feel they were too important and managed to skip out most nights. The summer just got longer for everyone, I was wishing to be back at work where I didn't have to deal with all of the drama that was being sent my way. I went to bed every night wondering what was next? I didn't have to wonder for too many nights before the next curve ball was thrown.

It was a hot summer and no one wanted to do their chores, I didn't either so I caved and made a deal with the girls. We would go to the pool during the day, after dinner they would clean their rooms. This seemed reasonable but when it came time for them to pay their price, I got ignored. The next day we all woke up and Noel thought we could renegotiate. I was tired of being taken advantage of, the only way any of the kids would take me seriously was if I had a break down and started crying. That still works on them and I still resort to that defense mechanism when I need to get their attention. I ended up grounding Noel for the weekend because she was completely disobeying our original agreement.

Our house didn't have air conditioning, just a swamp cooler. On this particular night, even that wasn't working. Noel asked if she could sleep in the basement because it was so much cooler. I agreed and then went to bed in my stuffy room upstairs. I woke up to the phone ringing and had to crawl over Mark to answer because he wasn't budging after the twelve pack that he drank before bed. There was a cop on the line asking me if I knew where my children were. I of course assumed it was Tony again in trouble. I replied that the kids were all safe and sound in the house and inquired what the call was about. Noel had snuck out to go meet her friends that lived up the block. There were five of them sitting on the retaining wall at the park when I arrived to pick her up along with the other parents. The kids got in trouble for breaking curfew and had to report to the detention center. Noel was the youngest at the age of twelve, her other friend was the same age and the other kids were in their teens. The detention center knew me by first name by the end of that summer between Tony and Noel going off the deep end.

CHAPTER 10

Growing Pains

S ummer of fright down in the books, none too soon. Noel had a court appearance for her curfew ticket. The judge gave her a fine and, a lecture and asked that she watch a movie. The movie was about a boy who broke the law and had an ankle bracelet for several weeks. Noel was to return a report to the judge about the movie and the impact it had on her. I am fairly sure there was little or no impact, but between the two kids that had been in trouble with the law that summer, this was the easier sentence to complete.

I worked on a school campus with a regular high school and a vocational high school. I currently worked at the vocational high school and was content. My boss asked if I would be interested in taking a full-time lead role in the financial department next door. The money was considerably better then what I was making so I was intrigued. I would miss the friends that I had made but would be right next door and could still see them at lunch. I applied and got the position, this high school was an alternative high school for students who did not fit in at a regular school. The students ranged from troubled teens to homeless to very wealthy spoiled kids that couldn't be bothered with a basic society. There was never a dull moment at that school between the alternative students and what I consider alternative staff, myself included.

An exciting time for me with the job change and Markie graduating that school year. I could hardly believe the time had passed so quickly with my little boy. Now applying for colleges around the country. I encouraged him to apply to five schools but he only had his sights set on the one he had wanted to go to since the age of ten. We would wait until wrestling season was starting before applying because I wanted to make sure he was scouted for possible scholarships through academics and sports. I would help him write his essays for the schools because he was more of a math and science guy, but I didn't look at it as cheating because everyone needs a little help at some point.

Mark was not terribly receptive to my school switch. He liked the bigger paycheck but didn't like that I would be with a whole new group of people. Mark was fine with me working at the school with Jamie, he thought if I had been up to something, he would have heard through John. How foolish, Jamie and I didn't share anything with either of those men. Mark felt the need to come help me move my one box of supplies from the old school to my new office. It was his way of stalking me and the people I would be working with every day. It took about two minutes for him to be in the office before he had a meltdown about the school counselor. I was giving Mark a tour through the school, we went in the clinic to find the counselor taking a nap. That escalated into people can just go in the clinic and do whatever they want, which in Mark's world meant I was sure to go in the clinic and snuggle up to the counselor while he was napping. Mark was getting more and more possessive now that I was out in the world with people other than my kids. I talked him off of his ledge by promising to show him how I can work and be a good wife to him when I got home. Just the idea makes me want to vomit. It was clear, we were growing apart. Not that he hadn't been pushing me in that direction for twenty years already.

I had a routine to get up early in the morning to avoid physical contact with Mark and hit the gym. I always told him I had to go so early because the kids would still be sleeping and I could get back to get everyone out the door for school before Mark left for work. Most mornings that worked, and I was getting in great shape trying to hide from him. I then would go to work, another place I felt safe from my home life. I wasn't sure what was happening, but I knew I was headed in the wrong direction with Mark. Truthfully, I had known that for a few years but the new job with a decent paycheck and benefits was fueling my desire to become independent. My friend Jamie was going to wait until their youngest was eighteen before she made her break. I hadn't contemplated if or when I would make a break but a girl can dream. I had a phone call on my office line every morning from Mark to make sure I was sitting at my desk. That call would be followed up by the lunch phone call and then one at the end of my work day. This was worse than being micromanaged by my boss. If I didn't answer right away, he would call my cell phone and accuse me of lying to him about where I was and who I was with. That is no way to live for him or me.

In the meantime, my kids were not in the know of what was happening with Mark and I because I never wanted them to see us at odds. I didn't think it was healthy for them to see their parents fighting all of the time. What they saw instead was their father telling me exactly what to do and who to speak to. Many times, I just would not say anything because everything I wanted to say would upset Mark and I was beginning to wonder what he would do if he got angry with me again. That is why my job and my friends at the gym were so important to me, I could be myself again. I was just starting to remember the person I was before I married Mark. I wasn't a coward, I had opinions and a good head on my shoulders. The last two decades he single-handedly worked to crush those traits, but I was getting them back, little by little. My growing pains would not stop me from being the best parent I could be without much help from the other parent.

In the past I had so much trouble with Tony's behavior that the one day I got a phone call from the principal about my son doing drugs on lunch break, I automatically was sure I would be picking Tony up. The principal informed me that Markie and his friends were spotted coming back to school from lunch smelling like marijuana and would be suspended due to the drug free school zone. I thought my head was going to explode at that moment. I drove down to the school and stormed in the office ready to rip Markie's head off. This was the week of the play offs for football and Markie was going to be named All City Corner Back. A big deal to some, monumental to Markie for his college resume.

Markie was in tears pleading that he didn't do drugs but the other kids did and he was getting suspended for nothing. I believed him because he wasn't that type of kid. I told the principal that I would be taking him to the drug test facility and testing him that afternoon. I thought if I could prove Markie wasn't lying then I would have fixed everything. We got in the car and off we went, an hour later I brought the negative test results back as proof for the principal and the football coach. They appreciated our efforts but still suspended Markie from school and the play-off game. This also meant the award that he was to be receiving would go to another student in the county. Drugs were ruining everyone around me whether they did them or not.

I managed to pull myself together, and move on with the plan of getting Markie scholarships as if the suspension never happened. It was wrestling season and this was going to be a make it or break it year. I had invested everything I could in Markie going to college on wrestling and he had given everything he could. He deserved a shot at getting out of the hell hole of our house and making a life for himself. One of us should escape and I had already made my bed, I made it a point to do what I could to help the kids get away.

Report cards were mailed home for the first quarter of the year. I had a good idea what they would look like, we would split the difference and half of them I would put on the fridge, the other half would be attached with a warning of failure letter. I was right, when I saw Tony's, I knew I would have to step in or he would not graduate on time or at all. Noel's wasn't much better but she was not at a place where she would be held back from anything, yet. I had her stay after school and work with a tutor until she was able to get her grades in check. Markie and Morgan were straight A students, I was so accustomed to their A's I hardly batted an eye. I explained to Tony that if he did not pull himself together and bring his grades up, not only would he not wrestle, but I would take him from the regular school and enroll him where I worked. He got his grades up just enough to wrestle most weeks, there were a couple that he sat out of the matches. It was bad for him and bad for the team, I did the helicopter mom thing and stepped in to clean up. I would let him finish the semester at his school and would have him transfer to the alternative school after Christmas break. He would still be able to wrestle for his original high school because my school didn't have an athletic department.

The kids were all getting burnt out with finals and practices by the time Christmas came around. I had this great idea of the family taking one last big vacation before Markie went to college. Mark liked my idea, the next step was to sell the kids. You wouldn't think it would be hard to sell kids on taking a vacation, but the proposal had some draw backs. I read the book Skipping Christmas and thought it was brilliant. We took the kids to a Mexican restaurant for dinner a couple weeks before Christmas and I pitched the idea of them giving up gifts that year, in return we would take them on an all-inclusive tropical vacation. No one jumped for joy at the thought of not getting presents but could see the big picture of how spring break would be spent. The family was hitting the beach in the middle of March, we started a count down.

The holidays passed quickly with only a passport stuffed by Santa in each stocking. Once New Years was over, it was back to focusing on getting Tony transferred and Markie ready to wrestle for a scholarship to his school of choice. Life was going accordingly with Markie, he remained healthy and wrestling well. Tony got to have all of my co-workers babysit him through each class, I was informed when he went to the bathroom. But as per preschool years, he excused himself to go to the bathroom and snuck out of the school. My boss gave him another chance as a favor to me and security on my jailbird became even tighter.

Wrestling season was a success for both boys. Tony was always eligible because the alternative school did not grade traditionally. Markie went to state and placed third. I was so proud of him because he was setting goals and accomplishing them one at a time. I see different wonderful things in each of my children, Markie's ability to make something happen is one that I love about him. A few weeks after the state finish, the coach of the college that Markie had wanted to attend gave us a call. We went to tour the campus and Markie was offered a partial scholarship for wrestling. It was too late to request an academic scholarship for that year but it didn't matter to us because he had been accepted, just as he had planned.

We were able to get our bags packed and really celebrate the family time together along with all of the new future plans that would be happening. I bought each kid a disposable camera to take pictures of what they thought was their version of the vacation. I look back on those pictures and find they reflect so much on the individual personalities. The trip was five days long and I had an activity planned if not two for every day. We snorkeled, did a sand buggy tour, went on a boat trip to a private island to go hiking and many other tourist things. This was turning out to be just how I had hoped, everyone was getting along and having fun with each other. There was plenty of beach time when the boys would take off and explore, while Mark and I would play in the ocean with the girls.

Morgan had been asking for a sombrero the whole vacation but we had been too busy to go out and look for one up until the last day. Our flight was not leaving until 6pm and our hotel stay was complete with check out at 11am. The night before we had all agreed to get up early to go souvenir shopping in the town. I gave each kid some spending money and picked a meeting place and time to avoid missing our flight. The boys took off in one direction and Mark took off in another. He hated shopping and said he was going to the beach while we were browsing and would meet back at the corner we had picked. I took the girls to get the sombrero, there were too many to choose from but we managed to pick the biggest and the most decorative hat. Everyone was back at the corner at the right time accept Mark. We had to get a cab back to the hotel to pick up our luggage and get to the airport two hours prior to our flight. It was only Noon, we had a little buffer in the event that something detained us. The kids and I waited over an hour on that corner and I started to panic. I was trying to hold myself together for the kids, but I knew something wasn't right.

I flagged down a police officer who had been circling the area, I did the best I could to explain that one of the people in our group was missing. Markie had been taking Spanish for a couple of years in high school and I found myself relying on his knowledge to get through some challenging moments on the trip. The officer took my information and asked us to go back to the hotel and wait for word from him or the American Consolette. I grabbed a cab and went back to the hotel, we were clearly not going to make our flight so I asked if I could have a late check out in one of the rooms. We put all of our luggage in one spot, I got the kids together and asked them not to worry and to get their suits on and go to the beach one last time before leaving. I then went to the hotel concierge and asked him to start calling all of the hospitals and jails in the area. About twenty minutes into our calls, the officer came by to get an identification of a man they found on the beach who seemed to be out of sorts. I ran down only to find the man wasn't Mark. The search was still on but I didn't know where to look.

Markie and Tony knew the severity of the situation and did their best to keep Noel and Morgan busy and happy. I went back up to the lobby disappointed and anxious about the choices I was going to have to make. The concierge had tracked down who we believed was

Mark in one of the local jails. I had no idea what he had done but I wasn't terribly surprised. I gathered up the kids, got them cleaned up and ready to leave the hotel. No matter what happened to Mark, my children were getting out of that country. We were in some kind of danger and I wasn't going to risk their lives over whatever Mark did to land in a foreign jail.

The cab driver pulled up and I asked him to take us to the jail that Mark was suspected to be held at. It was a somber drive and I had no choice but to drag the kids at this time. I planned to bail Mark out and go straight to the airport as a family. We pulled up to the jail and all bailed out of the cab, I wasn't going to take my eyes off of my kids, they were going to have to see the other side of their father whether he liked it or not. Once in the jail, the cab driver offered to interpret for us because Markie as good as he was at Spanish was not going to be able to navigate this discussion.

After the driver and the main desk officer got finished talking, I was told that I would need to get a lawyer to get Mark released. I couldn't imagine what he would have done that required a lawyer and was not yet given the charges of his crime. Conveniently enough, the driver's cousin, who just happened to be at that very jail was a lawyer. I didn't have much choice, I paid the damn lawyer and kept the driver to help with communications. I was being played in the worst way from the hotel concierge placing us with the driver who was related to the lawyer and so on and so on.

The lawyer was able to inform me that Mark was in jail because he was trying to buy drugs from someone on the beach but didn't realize it was part of a sting operation the police were conducting. In one minute, Mark ruined the vacation that was so wonderful. Once I processed what was going on I was told that due to Mark's crime he was no longer at that jail and had been transferred to a high security prison on the opposite side of the town. I pulled Markie and Tony aside and explained everything that was going on and made a decision for Markie to stay with me to help his father, while I send

Tony on a plane with the girls back to the states. Markie didn't want to stay, but he didn't argue. He just went along with the plan.

Noel and Morgan were crying and scared as we filed back into the cab, this time with our lawyer in tow. The first stop was to the ATM for a large withdraw from the one and only credit card I had left. I also had to call Terry and Jack to borrow money to be wired. Over all, I needed to come up with two thousand dollars to get Mark and leave the country. The clock was ticking and the kids were going to have to separate soon. I rolled the dice and kept them all together for one last shot at picking up Mark before sending them in a separate cab to the airport.

We arrived at the prison, it was frightening to be in the waiting area, I can't imagine what the cells were like, nor did I care to find out. The lawyer was in negotiations while I had to have Markie help me count the money. I was frazzled and couldn't do the conversion of pesos to American dollar amount without his help. One of the pictures Tony took with his camera was one of Markie and I counting money with the police symbol painting on the wall behind us. It is a very powerful picture representing the life I had chosen.

After a few minutes, Mark came out of the back of the building. He was filthy and smelled horrible but it was him and not some ghost I was chasing. I never had confirmation of his identity, I just took it on blind faith that I was going to see Mark, not some stranger. I paid the fines and the lawyer so we could all leave together. The cab driver was ready to drive at high speed to get us to the airport, our flight was leaving in an hour.

A screeching sound of the breaks woke the emotionally drained kids as we arrived outside the terminal. We all rushed through security as I begged and pleaded with the man going through our suitcases to hurry because we were going to miss our flight. He took his time and said we needed to run through the airport because the gate would soon be closing. All six of us were running on adrenaline, we made it to the gate a couple of minutes before they announced the flight was getting ready to leave. I went up to the counter and tapped on the person who was closing the gate, it was the man from security. I almost lost my mind and started screaming, but the look on the faces of my defeated children told me to ask politely if we would still be able to board the plane. We were able to catch the flight but couldn't sit together as a family. The boys had seats by each other and the girls were in seats a few rows away. That left me to sit with Mark, I couldn't bring myself to be next to him. I traded seats with Noel and took my chair next to Morgan. I just wanted to be home, I was so busy calming Morgan down, I hardly had time to focus on what I needed to do to change my life.

Home sweet home, I had never been so happy to see our house and our neighborhood. Markie stated he would never leave the United States again. The other kids didn't speak much of what happened, I think to them it was more of a nightmare they didn't care to remember. I processed the film from their cameras and had everything from the beautiful ocean to the poverty of the town and of course the infamous police station picture. This was the end of my Norman Rockwell dreams, something had to be done, it was bad enough that Mark was ruining his life, but he was taking us with him, I had to decide what to do and how much damage it would truly cause.

CHAPTER 11

Time After Time

Cyndi Lauper doesn't realize the impact her song, "Time After Time" has on my kids and I. On long road trips I used to play this song among other 80's greats, but particularly this song. The kids would chime in and sing with me until one day we deemed this our family song. Not the whole family, Mark was too cool to sing music from back in the day. I played it even more for us to belt out because of that.

Senior year was coming to a close, I had mixed emotions about Markie leaving the nest because I would miss him but I also knew he would be better off getting out of that house. Things were not good with Mark and I after the return of our family trip. I was tired of his selfish ways constantly hurting the rest of us, but I still tried to maintain the lie that everything would be fine for the kids' sake. I knew I wanted out, I just wasn't sure how to make that happen. In Markie's senior year book, I was able to submit a baby picture and a caption for him to reflect on. I chose words from our family song, "If you're lost, you can look, you will find me. Time after time." I would always be there for all four of my babies even if it didn't always feel like that to them.

So many exciting things coming up with graduation for Markie and at my work. I was a big part of the graduation ceremony that my school held every year. It was also the beginning of softball season. The girls had both traded in their leotards and ballet slippers for cleats and bats. Each girl was on a competitive team that took them to opposite ends of Colorado every weekend. Mark and I had to split up to get one or the other of the girls to their tournaments. This worked out perfect for me because I almost never had to see Mark on the weekends then right back into the weekly work routine.

At work I had become great friends with one of the other girls who worked on the third floor. Angie was a single parent of two who lived with her mother to make life easier monetarily and for child care. She was a good friend to me for a long time but Mark couldn't stand her, not because she had ever done anything to him but because he felt threatened by her friendship. Mark stated several times that Angie was corrupting me into thinking being a single parent was glamorous and how I should try it. I was never under the impression her life was anything but hard, if anything it frightened me into staying with Mark longer.

Angie helped me plan the graduation party that we would throw for Markie and his cousin. They were graduating from different high schools but were both attending the same college. It was fitting to have them share a party in celebration of their accomplishments. I was off on a party planning mission when I got a call that Mark had taken a fall on his dirt bike. He had torn his ACL and would need surgery. At that time, I was also trying to talk Mark into letting me trade my car for a jeep. Another sign that the old me was fighting to come out. Mark put his foot down and refused to allow me to look for a jeep or any vehicle. I explained that I would pay for it with my own paycheck and he would not have to do a thing accept cosign the loan. I gave up on the idea, but not for long. I was going to get a jeep and Mark was going to sign the loan.

A couple of weeks down the road, Mark was scheduled for his knee surgery. An out-patient procedure that would only take a few hours. I had half a mind to leave as soon as I dropped him off, considering that is what he did when I had my teeth pulled so many years before. I stayed and concocted "operation buy jeep" plan. The doctor wheeled Mark out for me to take home, he was completely out of it. Not to the point that I had to carry him, to the point that I could manipulate him into thinking he wanted to buy a jeep. I went to the pharmacy, gave him his prescribed medications and drove right to the car dealership. Mark was not in a place to argue, he signed the papers and we drove home in my new 2009 four door Wrangler.

The next morning, Mark was still groggy. I thanked him for coming around to my way of thinking and letting me get the jeep because of all of the driving I would be doing for softball with the girls. He never knew what hit him, I assumed I would have to start playing dirty, the jeep was a good test of what I was working with as an opponent.

The graduation was getting closer but the boys had to get through prom first. They both had girlfriends that I loved. I watched Markie's girl take control of the relationship, I wasn't thrilled about that but he was a pretty happy go lucky guy and needed a little kick in the butt on occasion. Prom night came and he had a black tuxedo with red tie and cumber bun to match his date's dress. However, he loves baseball hats and insisted on wearing a hat. I went to take pictures at one of the other friends' house along with his girlfriend's parents. Her mother had the audacity to tell my son to take his hat off. I intervened with a compromise, some of the pictures will be with the hat and some without. The mother wasn't pleased but it wasn't really her call. Imagine, moms interfering in their kids' lives, well I never...

Tony also was getting ready for prom, his girlfriend was so sweet, I watched him walk all over her the way Mark did to me. I would interfere but that would be to save her from turning into me. Just like I did, Tony's girlfriend turned a cheek to the drug problems as if it wasn't happening. Both the boys off to prom in the rain, they would see each other that night and act as if they had never met. Tony was becoming estranged from Markie one day at a time. I don't know if it was the because he knew Markie was leaving or if the drugs were taking over his life, perhaps both.

The boys made it through prom, even with their mom sitting at the after prom dealing black jack to a bunch of high school students. Another week of finals and the year would be complete. Tony did not have finals at the alternative school and was so far back on track to graduate the following year on time. Mark's younger sister and older brother did not graduate from high school, this was a big thing for me, I struggled but I made it and I would move heaven and earth to see all four of my kids with diplomas.

Both sides of the family were at Markie's graduation. It was a hot day in late May but I didn't care because he had made it through this chapter and had so many more to look forward to. I cried when he walked across the stage. In the blink of my eyes the graduation was done and it was time to celebrate. Our party wasn't until the weekend which enabled us to go to all of the other parties. I had watched all of these boys and girls grow up and was secretly jealous of the new beginnings ahead of them, I missed that window but I am the one who closed it.

Our party was a success and didn't down pour until the very end. Angie was there to help out regardless of how Mark felt about her. I was thankful to have any help that I could get because I knew I would be dealing with an intoxicated Mark for the evening. Markie raked in enough money to buy a lap top for college, this was a huge relief for me knowing all of the other expenses that would come with school.

I was off for the summer, running the girls around to games and sleepovers all of the time. Markie was working at the stadium again but Tony was not able to work there because of his previous violation. I started to notice my things went missing, I didn't want to think that my own child could steal things from his own family so I blamed his reckless friends. I was only partially right, Tony would tell his friends what to take and where it was so he wouldn't feel so guilty. Tony didn't work that summer, he became a thief to fund his drug use. Tony no longer was using pain killers as his addiction had taken him to a new level, he now was into heroin. I didn't know that at the time and had little patience for theft in my own home. My mother's antique emerald rings were both gone among so many other things. I had enough of the behavior and couldn't keep putting the other kids in danger of what Tony would do next. I kicked him out of the house and didn't think twice about it. Mark was fine with the decision because Tony had figured out how to break into the newest garden to sell off profits. Mark was furious when he figured out that Tony had been breaking into what used to be our family camper, now Mark's green house.

Tony went to his best friend's house, I only know this because the mom called to let me know Tony was safe and sound. The kid was a 17-year thief, his having a nice cozy place to stay wasn't on the top of my lists of worries. The only thing that changed was the house they were stealing from to do drugs. One night, Tony got picked up by the cops for being out past curfew. My kids sure had a hard time obeying that law when they were underage. The cops brought him back home, I tried to refuse that he be left there. I was threatened by the officer to have me and Mark arrested for parental neglect, it turns out it is against the law to kick your kid out before the age of eighteen. Once I was told that I broke down and started crying, it would be a very long year if I had to tolerate Tony under my own roof. I really thought if he were forced to grow up, he would stop doing drugs and get a job. Life would get better for him and the rest of the family and everything would be fine. The reality was that things were never going to be fine as long as we all continued as if nothing was wrong.

I didn't know what to do about Tony, I asked my sister but she didn't have the answers either. All four of her kids were such well-behaved, respectful people. Where did I go wrong with this kid? It was up to me to fix him, this is one thing I couldn't quit on. I took him to our pediatrician and got the names of some counseling programs that might help. Tony was always so charming, he could lie to your face and you would leave believing every word he said. I was always giving him money for fear that he would steal something else from someone else. I enabled him his entire life and this was no different, I wanted to sweep our issues under a rug, that summer I did just that, I worked harder on keeping my family functioning then I did helping Tony. My regrets just keep adding up.

Needless to say, the situation in our household was becoming more intolerable. I approached Mark one evening and explained to him that I wasn't happy. That was the last thing he cared to hear about, he was trying to start a larger growing operation and all of a sudden, my friend Angie who he hated became someone of interest. Angie lived over in a little house that she could no longer afford the rent on and needed to move. When Mark got wind of this, he had this idea of renting the house out and turning it into a more lucrative business. His idea was to produce enough pot to sell to pay for Markie's college. I wasn't going to send my son to school on drug money so I was against this idea 100%. Mark never listened to what I thought was the right thing to do and moved forward with his business. One of his construction co-workers was in on the job. That person stayed at the house to take care of all of the maintenance involved at night and Mark would go over during his work hours through-out the day. He was the foreman and was able to mysteriously vanish for hours at a time without question. His crew was happy getting paid and didn't care what he did with his time.

My complaints went by the waist side with Mark, his way of trying to fix our problems was to leave town again. Another trip to Sturgis, but we would be renting a huge RV that his sister and I would trade off driving while Mark and his brother in law rode their bikes a head. I didn't want to go, I didn't want to leave my kids. I was afraid of the boys having a party or getting into trouble. I got some advice from a therapist that I had gone to through work. I didn't tell anyone I was seeing her and my work only covered three appointments per person unless you invited your family or spouse, then you could get a fourth session. I told her how much I was struggling with my marriage and that Mark wanted to go out of town again. I wasn't comfortable leaving with him because this would have given him the perfect chance to make me disappear. Sturgis has too many moving parts to worry about one plain mom from the suburbs. I knew I had to be on my best behavior if I went. The therapist thought it might give Mark and I a chance without all of the stresses of home around to reconnect with each other. I had already disconnected but wasn't going to be the one blamed when our family crumbled, I agreed to go on the trip. We would go for a long weekend and the following weekend move our son into college.

The motorcycle rally was in August just before the start of school. There were no classes in session but the staff needed to be in to prep for the students return in a couple of weeks. I came home from work on a Thursday and got my bag packed to hit the road the next morning. I packed shorts and t-shirts and a couple of suits for swimming if we got to stop at a pool or go to a lake. I was able to fill a suitcase instead of grabbing a pair of jeans like the last trip to Sturgis. Mark got home from work and went through my suitcase. He picked it up and dumped it on the floor, I thought he was mad because my shorts were too short or the shirts were too revealing. He went through all of my clothes and found the smallest things I had and packed them in the suitcase. I never threw clothes out so I actually had some things from several years ago that I thought were ok to wear but he said were slutty. They were now packed along with high heels that I never wore and a pair of tall black boots. I asked why he was packing all of the things he hated and he said he would be dressing me for the weekend because he needed me to fit in with the other biker girls. I knew this was going to be an awful trip but it was too late now, he wasn't in his right mind and I wasn't crossing him.

The four of us met up to rent our RV just outside of town on the way to Sturgis. Mark's sister offered to drive first which I was happy about because this was a way bigger vehicle than I had ever driven. I don't claim to be the best driver so this thing freaked me out. We all loaded our things in, I had bought food and alcohol for the trip to save us some money while we were there. Loaded and ready to roll, we took off following the bikes. I had never gotten along with Mark's family very good so sitting in a vehicle with his sister was painful. I talked about everything just to avoid the awkward silence, I am pretty good at just listening to myself talk when no one else contributes to the conversation.

After half a day of driving, we finally arrived at our campsite. We stayed at the Buffalo Chip, not the highest end place but that is where we stayed the year before and the concerts held there were fantastic. On this trip we would see several different concerts and ride up to the stage in the front row with the bikes. We took a day ride to Mt. Rushmore and through the Badlands, both were simply breath taking. During the day I would be dressed in jeans a tank top and motorcycle boots, at night for the shows I would be dressed in little or nothing and told to look down and to not make eye contact. The hate was building in me but I was in no place to voice my feelings. I almost made it through the weekend without too many setbacks, but on the last night we all wanted to go into town to a bar called the Full Throttle. This was a hot spot during bike week and we had to check it out. It was dirty but everything out there was a temporary build, this was a huge dwelling that served booze and let bikers do burnouts. Once we were done at the bar we headed back to camp to catch the concert, I hopped on the back and off Mark went. As we came to a turn just out of the parking lot, he tried to do a burn out with me on the back and I went flying off the bike. Thankfully, I wasn't hurt, just a few bumps and bruises on my legs and arms. We never rode with helmets so I am grateful this accident wasn't worse. Mark's first instinct was to pick me up and get out of there before the cops showed up. We got back to camp to clean my wounds, then went out. I had several drinks and was furious for the lack of concern when I was dumped off of the bike. My mouth was going to get me in trouble, I knew it but couldn't hold it in anymore.

After the concert and a few more beverages, we went to a club that was on site at the campground. I was dancing and having fun until a song came on that Mark hated. I was singing as loud as I could but didn't care, everyone else but Mark was too. He came across the dance floor, grabbed me by the hair and dragged me out of the club. I was screaming, no one cared, everyone there minded their own business as if to say this was acceptable behavior. I was dragged all the way to the RV before Mark would speak. I was told I act like a slut and no wife of his would make him look so stupid. I screamed back because I knew his brother in law wasn't far behind and would hopefully step in. Mark raised his hand just as his sister opened the door. I hadn't seen that look since we were kids and I knew we weren't going to recover from his anger forever. His sister may have calmed him down then but what would happen the next time he turned to rage?

The next morning, Mark was apologetic. It was too late for me. His apologies meant nothing. I just wanted to get home. I called the boys on the way in to town giving them a solid two-hour warning if they needed to clean up after entertaining. I drove Mark's sister and I in silence, there was nothing for me to say. She had seen how he was towards me and didn't have any words in his defense or any words of comfort to me. After returning the RV and parting ways, we rode home on the back of the bike, just enough background noise to avoid conversations. We both new things were coming to an end, it was just a matter of how long.

Shockingly, the boys got the hint to clean up after the party they had the night before. The neighbor tipped me off before I got home, he was a younger guy and didn't want to rat the boys out to the police but he was sure to tell me. I yelled and screamed a little but had other things on my mind.

Mark and I slept in the same room but that was going to change. I got up and went to the gym and then off to work. I knew Mark would call to make sure I hadn't left the country or lied about anything. I took that call as an opportunity to tell him that I thought we needed to go to counseling to help resolve our marital issues. I wasn't invested in the idea, but another suggestion made by the therapist, I thought it couldn't hurt. I had my mind made up but I wanted validation of how bad I had been treated through the years and seeing a therapist was my way of achieving that validation. Mark refused to go to a therapist, he thought it was ridiculous to involve someone else in our personal issues. His opinion of this was based on the one time I asked him to see the therapist when I was a teenager. I didn't care, I was going to leave him with or without the therapy.

I came home to a dozen roses on the counter and a very remorseful husband. I thanked him for the gesture and let him know that Steve's wife was coming over to watch a new show that we had been dying to see. I figured he would be over at his other house working on his drug operation and it wouldn't matter. Sure enough, after dinner he left just as Melonie was walking in with a bottle of wine. I was not a big drinker for most of the years the kids were little, but lately I had been having drinks just to get through my day. The kids were old enough to take care of themselves for the most part so I didn't see the harm in a drink here and there. Noel plopped down on the couch in between Melonie and I for the show. It was called "Cougar Town", we wanted to watch it because of the actors. Melonie and I had watched every episode of "Friends" and were thrilled to see some of the characters were in the new show. Just as the show was ending and we were finishing our wine, Mark came home. He walked in the kitchen that was connected to the living room and asked what the show was about. I said a forty-year-old woman who was starting over. Mark asked Noel the name of the show and he went berserk.

Melonie grabbed what was left of the wine and ran out the house saying she would call me later and thanks for hanging out. Noel started to see how bad her dad could be towards me. Mark swiped his hand across the table where the flowers were perfectly arranged in a crystal vase and sent the flowers flying through the air and glass shattering all over the floor. I rushed Noel off to her room and felt relief that the other kids were in their rooms not paying attention. Mark was sure the show was the bible to becoming a cougar and how I wanted to be with younger men. He stormed out of the house after he made a spectacle of himself in front of our teenage daughter.

I didn't bother to clean up, I needed to make sure Noel was not flipping out. She was so upset because she thought it was her fault for telling her dad the name of the show. I hated him more and more every day. Noel was at a very impressionable age being thirteen and in seventh grade. She was very smart about reading people and asked if her dad and I were going to get a divorce. I didn't have a clear answer or the guts to say yes at that time.

Mark came home drunk as usual late that night, fortunately for me, he passed out with his clothes on and didn't bother me. I snuck out to go to the gym and waited extra-long to avoid him that morning. I just had to get through moving Markie to college in two days and then I would start making arrangements to leave the house myself. I had already talked to Terry and was able to crash on her couch until I could get the divorce process going. The one set back would be the three kids that were left at home with a maniac. If Mark would calm down and accept his fate then we would be able to help the kids understand what was going to happen.

I did my best to avoid or not speak to Mark by working and running the girls to practices or after school activities. Markie was floating on a cloud because he was about to be on his own and he couldn't wait. The whole family got up early that Saturday morning to start packing his truck and our truck full of things he would want or need to have in his dorm. I am a person that over packs and I spared no expense in how much stuff I was making Markie take. I was so proud and sad at the same time to have one of the kids leaving home but I would never say that to Markie because I wanted him to bask in all of the experiences without the guilt of his weeping mother. Markie assured me he would be home the following week to do laundry and have a home cooked meal.

The next few days were somber to me without Markie in the house. He was never home but he was home just enough to feel his presence. I didn't bother him, not because I didn't want to know what was going on but the parent meeting that I had to attend for his school asked that we leave the kids alone to give them time to adjust. Markie adjusted flawlessly, if he wanted to come home he did, most of the time he was too busy with classes and the team along with finding time to see his girlfriend who was going to a school further away. Mark would give me a hard time about Markie leaving because he knew it was hard for me to let go. Mark also agreed that we needed therapy and he was willing to hear what I had to say in front of a stranger. This was a game to him, it was a game I would play for a short time and then a game he would lose.

I scheduled an appointment with the therapist I had been seeing for the next afternoon. The ride in the jeep was quiet on the way there because Mark didn't know what to expect. After the introductions, the therapist dove right into the questions. Mark started to get more and more angry, he was sure that I had told a bunch of lies to the doctor once he found out I had been there before. The therapist looked right at Mark and stated that he mentally abuses people and has a history of physical abuse. He denied the allegations, however, my nose is a clear reminder of what he was capable of if he got mad enough.

We left before our hour was up with Mark in a rage babbling about finding a therapist that would listen to him and see how hard he has had it being married to me all those years. I agreed to see someone he was comfortable with, he made an appointment two days later. I was losing my mind and starting to be mean back to him in front of the kids because I needed them to see how I had been living. I did such a good job of hiding things from them a split would come as a shock to all of them, accept maybe Noel.

Back in the jeep again for the next session. Mark and I went in and introduced ourselves to a therapist who was middle aged and very classic in appearance. Her office was put together by an interior designer, or that is how looked to me. Compared to the therapist that was provided by the school district, who had an office in an old temporary classroom outside of a rundown playground. Mark immediately started spewing my faults, he didn't hold back and I let him run with it. If I had a tape recorder for this session I would have played it back to him so that he could see what an ass he is. When it was my turn to talk, I explained a handful of things that had made me lose sight of why I married him and how I was tired of trying to please him or to be pleased.

After much banter back and forth between each of us and the therapist, she looked him dead in the face and called him an abuser. The suggestion this time was to come back in a week after we had a conversation with the kids about us separating and that we would try to work on our issues in therapy together. Mark stood up and said he would not come back to such an offensive person and we would not be separating, then promptly walked out.

I was being a martyr at this point but staying the course of the original suggesting of giving our marriage all that I had, I offered to pick a third therapist. I explained to Mark that some therapist doesn't fit every personality and we just needed to find one that would fit his personality. I sounded like my child hood therapist, Dr. Benson at that moment. I chuckled to myself about all of the sessions I had sat through in my life and yet here I was, practically middle aged still in therapy. Mark agreed to another doctor and I set one more appointment but I said it would be only on the stipulation that we have a family meeting when Markie got home that weekend to tell them we were separating. Mark was fine with that because he thought he was pacifying me until he would just force me to stay.

Third time is a charm, for me, not for Mark. The third doctor, third session and third accusation of being an abuser. It occurred to me that each time we were in these offices telling our life story that I was going to have to look at Mark and tell him I don't love him in order to get him to let me go. I would hold off on that as much as I could because I knew he would not react well. That night we went home and I decided to go out with my friend Angie who I had been forbidden to see other than at work when I had to. I no longer cared, I jumped in the jeep and left. I knew Mark would be going to the other house to tend to his precious plants and would come home smashed after I was already safely in bed. I wanted to grab a drink and discuss just how to tell my kids about our family not being the same as in the past. Angie had already been through it, I thought she was a good sounding board and drinking buddy.

I was getting ready for our family dinner and catching up with Markie. I knew how each child would take the news of our separation. I was planning on filing for divorce but I would play this game for a while because I needed to get some ducks in order before completely pulling the plug. Everyone was happy to have Markie back for the short time he would be there. After dinner and all of the teasing and laughing, I stood up and announced that their father and I wanted to talk to them all together. On que, Noel asked if we were getting a divorce. The boys threw food at her and told her to shut up. Tony thought we were planning our next vacation, Markie thought we were honoring him for some other terrific thing he had accomplished, and poor little innocent Morgan thought we were getting a new pet. This news was going to knock them down and it would be up to me to pick them up and dust them off, the same way I would do for myself.

I tried to finish my sentence before all of the interruptions but Mark beat me to the punch. He voiced loudly, "Your mother would like a separation and will be leaving to stay with her sister." My children looked at me in disbelief and started crying. Every one of them with tears in their eyes could not process what would have been so bad that I would want to leave them and the home I had created. I didn't want to leave, I wanted him to leave but I couldn't tell them that because they would never understand what I meant until one day they got to see the side of their father that I had known all those years.

Tony blamed himself and his drug addiction that we faced every single day. Morgan was just in shock and couldn't speak. I pulled Markie to the side to ensure him that I would take care of all of his school needs because I wanted him to succeed and not worry about not being able to stay at his school because of the cost. I made a promise to that boy that day and I kept my promise. Noel was upset but understood to some degree why I couldn't live with that man anymore. It would just be temporary, I would find a way to get full custody and the house back and he could figure out who's couch he would land on. Mark led them to believe everything would be fine after our little break and things would be back to normal.

The kids settled in for the night and I packed a bag. I was going to stay at Terry's that night, I couldn't do one more night in that house with Mark. I had always thought he was a good father for the most part, I know he loved the kids, they were old enough now to look out for each other and I would be around the block and a phone call away. I was just sleeping at Terry's, once Mark left for work I would come home and do what I had always done, take care of business.

I went to Terry and Jack's and told them about the dinner and how the kids were doing. They love the kids and all of the cousins are so close their family said they would make sure to keep an eye on how my kids were doing. Terry only had two kids at home at that time so I wasn't bothering their family schedule too terribly. While I was getting ready for bed, Mark called my cell phone to let me know he had thrown all of my thing on the front lawn. I called his mother right away because she was the only person he would listen to in a fit of rage. Elizabeth was nasty as always to me but I didn't care, I told her to help him for his own good and the safety of my kids. Terry and Jack went and grabbed the girls and brought them to me. The three of us slept on the pull out together afraid to let go of each other.

CHAPTER 12

Black Friday

I didn't sleep much the night I tried to move out of the house. I lay awake trying to figure out what I was going to do to make the divorce happen smoothly. It was obvious to both sides of the family that we were not going to fix our broken marriage. I just wanted to make things as painless as possible for the kids. I got the girls off to school and went into work, I skipped the gym because of sheer exhaustion. As always, I got a phone call from Mark, this time apologizing for his behavior. I used this to my advantage, the girls weren't safe in that house with him right now. I told Mark I would be willing to sleep on the couch through the holidays and then in the New Year would be filing for divorce. He didn't hear or listen to the divorce part, he just heard the part where I would be home.

The school secretary overheard my heated discussion with Mark and asked me to come in her office and shut the door. Sherrie had been through an ugly divorce to her first husband and had her second husband pass away. She knew what I was going through and offered to help. The office was small and everyone could hear all of the other conversations if they tried hard enough. Sherrie had been listening to my end of the conversation for months when I would have to answer and explain my where bouts to Mark. I told Sherrie I was going to file for divorce after the holidays, I was just trying to get the kids through without ruining Christmas. I also needed to save money for a lawyer, the retainers were an average of five thousand dollars. Sherrie suggested that I go get my own checking account started and have my paycheck direct deposited into that account instead of the joint account. My boss knew what was going on too because I was either mad or crying all of the time. I was able to leave work early that day, just after Tony was let out so he wouldn't say anything to his father about me not being at work. I waited for the daily afternoon phone call from Mark and then went to the bank. I opened my own account and would start depositing money as soon as I got paid. I only received a pay check the last day of the month so I would have to wait. In the meantime, I would keep paying bills out of the joint account.

The bank took longer than anticipated, I got home late. Mark is usually taking a nap while he waits for dinner to be put on the table and then off to his farm. This time he was waiting for me to get home. He insisted on searching my purse, he told me he didn't trust me because he received an anonymous text that I was with a man. If the banker counts, I was with a man. Mark trusting me was a non-issue, I didn't care how he felt. He found the temporary check book with my new account information. I was happy Tony was just getting home, otherwise I am not sure what Mark would have done. He was screaming at me at the top of his lungs, as soon as he saw Tony, Mark made some derogatory statement about what an awful person his mother is and to never be with a girl like that. It's no wonder Tony is not terribly respectful to girls; his role model is nothing but negative.

I blame Mark for Tony's drug addiction for that reason among others. Mark was always negative when Markie and Tony didn't do something right in sports or school. A kid can only be called lazy or stupid so much before it sets in the head. It also doesn't help that Mark is into drugs and is no longer hiding that fact because the kids are old enough to understand what he is doing. I will never understand what he is doing, I don't know why he would think they could.

Mark left and I was able to have some peace in the house. I tried to keep things as normal as possible for the girls. Tony was hardly around until it was time for me to drag him to school. I got him a bus pass to get home from school so he wouldn't have to wait for me to finish my work day to catch a ride. Tony was struggling to stay awake in classes and my coworkers were getting concerned about his health and his grades. He was slipping and only had through the end of the year before graduation, he was getting so close I hated to have him blow everything I had pushed him towards. Angie started buying him energy drinks to keep him awake and motivated to participate in class.

Noel was starting to act out in class, especially with the male teachers. They would assign homework and she would tell them she wouldn't be doing the work because no man would tell her how to act. I got a phone call from the principal letting me know that Noel would be suspended if she continued to behave so disrespectful. I went up and explained the situation to the principal, he understood we were dealing with a lot of emotional issues as a family. The principal had Noel see the school counselor once a week to help her work through her feelings. More and more it was obvious Noel was trying hard not to be like me, a shell of a woman.

I worked extra hard to let Morgan see how everything would be fine and that both her father and I loved her no matter what happened between us. Morgan and Markie internalize their feelings and both have stomach issues because of it. I asked if they would like to talk to someone and they both declined. Markie was already and adult I couldn't make him go to a therapist, I should have made Morgan go, it couldn't have hurt. I let her decide, she was ten already and I thought I would give her the choice.

Every night I would make dinner, Mark would leave and I would be asleep or faking sleep on the couch when he would come home drunk off his ass. Life was crawling by and I was feeling the sting of everything I would be dealing with in the coming months. The girls were playing basketball and were busy with friends, this was best for them to be around people and families that didn't have all of the hate towards each other. Thanksgiving was only a couple weeks away and our extended families were making plans. I refused to go to Mark's parents for their regular early dinner, I was going to my sister's house. Mark wasn't planning on attending my family functions either, at this point, my family couldn't stand the sight of him.

I had the week of Thanksgiving off of work and thought it would be good to get some things taken care of for my move. I hadn't been paid for the month so it would be hard to go out and buy anything I needed to start over until I got paid. I organized my things to be ready to throw them in boxes and leave as soon as I found the right time. Mark was being reasonably civil this week and suggested that we go get the kids all of their Christmas presents on Black Friday. I agreed to do this because I could have him pay and that would leave my pay check for the things I needed. Markie came home for the week because the school dorms were shut down during holidays and wresting was on hold until the new year. It would be so good to have him home again, even if just for a few days.

The morning of Thanksgiving I made the side dishes that I was asked to bring to Terry's and what I had always contributed to Mark's parents. The kids went with me for a little bit to visit their cousins at Terry's and then got called to go down to Elizabeth's for dinner. It was a moment that I remember and thought once we were divorced the kids' holidays will never be the same and they will always get pulled in different directions. I kept telling myself this would be the best thing for all of us eventually. I hung out at Terry's house for a few hours and then went home to make a list of gifts to buy. I was going to get my families gifts while we were out spending Mark's money.

My alarm went off at four in the morning to get up and hit the sales. I had done this in the past with Jaimie and had such a blast finding deals and people watching. I was concerned that this shopping experience wouldn't be so pleasant. I had made plans with friends from work to have drinks that night, I focused on that as my reward for spending the day with Mark. The girls were going to sleep overs and the boys were going to parties with their girlfriends. Mark and I drove in silence to the first store, I bought as many gifts as I could cross off of the list at that store in order to keep the shopping spree to a minimum. While we were in the cooking section finding a gift for Jack who is an amazing chef, Mark suggested I pick out some cookware because I would need it when I moved out. I thought it was odd, but I threw some stuff in the cart, I would take what I could get out this. Mark kept racking up our charge card because we had agreed to file bankruptcy before we filed our taxes. We were deep in debt and were going to lose the house. One more thing that we kept from the kids, they didn't need to know we were broke and practically homeless. The bankruptcy was to help keep the house long enough to put it on the market and walk away not owing.

Six hours after we started, we were home unloading all of the gifts for the kids and both families. We had a spot in our attic that we would hide them, our kids were always so good at snooping through the presents. I won't even put them out wrapped under the tree until Christmas morning because they try to shake every box. I had just enough time to take a nap before going out with my friend Tanya. After my very short nap that I got to take only because Mark was already over at his other house, I ran the girls to their sleepover. They were headed to the same house which was unusual but nice for a change.

Dressed and ready to head out the door, I was greeted by several of Markie's friends, they were all getting together and our house was the meeting spot. I gave a wave and drove away happy to be seeing the house in my review mirror. I arrived at one of my new hangouts, Baker's Street Pub. It was close and had a great happy hour. Tanya and I thought a couple other friends from work were going to show up but everyone was committed to family stuff. We didn't care we started drinking and visiting about what my life was going to look like in a few months. There were a couple of younger guys sitting next to us at the bar that started chatting us up. They suggested we go across the street and go bowling, I didn't have anything better to do and I was in no hurry to get home so we took them up on the offer. We had a lot of fun but I drank way too much and was ready to head home. Tanya knew I was going to be sick, we said our goodbyes and got out of there before I made a spectacle of myself. I couldn't even walk and got right by the jeep and started throwing up everywhere. I knew I couldn't drive and it was late, I called Markie to come pick me up. He and his girlfriend were there in ten minutes, Tanya made sure I wasn't alone until my ride arrived and then she drove off. Markie drove the jeep while his girlfriend followed in his truck.

At home I saw that only Tony was in the basement, everyone else had left and Mark wasn't home. I went up to my room to get my pajamas and robe on and to clean myself up. I was starting to feel better and would be just fine once I laid on the couch. Markie and his girlfriend went to his room in the basement and I passed out. I don't know how much time passed but I was awoken to the feeling of being ripped off the couch by my hair and dragged up the stairs to the master bedroom. At first, I didn't know what was going on because I was still out of it from the alcohol. In a sobering minute I knew that Mark was completely drunk and was very angry. He said I would not be getting a divorce and I would start acting like his wife again or he would kill me. I started to scream but he put the pillow over my face to muzzle the noise. I was sure this was how I was going to die, I begged through the pillow to stop but he just kept hitting and kicking me. He finally threw the pillow off of me but when I cried out for the boys he started to choke me. He ripped my pajamas off of me, I kept screaming "No" as loud as I could but he was still choking me with one hand while taking off his pants with the other hand. He let go of my neck and then rolled me to my stomach, I couldn't stop him from touching me, I fought with everything I had in me. After minutes of this I went limp, I had no fight left. As I accepted that I was going to die, my kids' faces flashed in my mind, I couldn't give up and leave them with this monster. I still had my robe on, Mark had a hold on the material and I started to tell him I would change and be the wife he wanted and that I loved him. It made me sick to say but it saved my life. He relaxed for a brief moment thinking he had won, I slipped out of my robe and ran naked as fast as I could to the basement screaming for help. Tony was the first to hear me, I told him to call the police and leave the lights off until I could get a shirt of his laying on the floor to cover myself. I didn't know how bad I had been hurt and I didn't want them to see me this way.

Markie and his girlfriend came running into Tony's room to find out what was going on, I took the phone and explained that my husband had tried to kill me and my sons and I weren't safe. I had to stay on the line with dispatch until the cops showed up. I asked Markie to call Terry and Jack and tell them I needed them right away. Tony ran upstairs to see his dad, Mark was getting his gun out of the gun cabinet. Tony didn't know what was going on, but he felt like he had to protect his father from the police. Tony watched his father jump off the balcony connected to our bedroom and run through the back gate.

When the police arrived, they came into search the house because I wasn't going to go upstairs until they got Mark. I had told them my younger son was sitting with him until they arrived, I thought that is what was happening, I had no idea Mark was gone. The boys and Markie's girlfriend had to go through a line of questioning. Jack stayed with them while Terry rode with me to the hospital. I had to have a rape kit along with all of the bruises and lacerations checked and documented. I kept waiting to hear if Mark was in jail, he was on the run and considered armed and dangerous. I called his mother to let her know what had happened.

I don't know how I didn't die that night completely but some part of me is defiantly dead and Mark is the one who killed me, slowly over time. The lower half of my body was covered in bruises and my neck covered in red marks and scratches. I hated having to go home to my kids looking the way I did, but someone was going to have to be there for them and I wasn't going to let Mark be any part.

Terry called the house of the girl's sleepover and explained that we had a family emergency and needed the girls to stay a while longer. The police would not let me go back to my home and asked the boys to get some things and stay with Terry and Jack until we were safe. Mark was on the run and had not been found, it had already been twelve hours since his escape with no idea of where he might be. Markie and Tony were not happy to leave their home and Markie's girlfriend was now a part of the investigation which made her parents dislike us even more than before.

Terry and I pulled up to her house where my kids were waiting for me, I didn't want to face them, I didn't want to face any one. I had no choice, I had to grow up and take care of the only things that mattered to me and the four faces that got me through the scariest night of my life. The boys didn't know everything that happened because the police had us in different rooms for questioning. On that day, they were happy to see me and vowed to protect me, they just couldn't believe they were having to protect me from their father.

I called Angie later that night because she had been calling and calling, she knew something was wrong because Tanya had told her I had Markie come get me from the bowling alley. In a matter of an hour Angie and Tanya were at my sister's house trying to make sure I was doing ok. I laid on the couch in pain and just cried, I didn't have words for what had happened. A few minutes after they left, the girls were brought to the house. I didn't give them the whole truth, just that dad got angry and left the house but isn't feeling well and needed some time away from all of us. I told them we were letting him stay at the house and that he would visit when he was feeling better.

Markie went back to college and Tony went to his friend's house to stay. The girls and I stayed for three more nights before Mark got locked up. His brother Steve was hiding him, Mark ended up turning himself in because his mother told him he had to or things would be much worse for him in the long run.

I took a call from the detective informing me that Mark had turned himself in and was now in custody. We were safe to go home, they felt there was enough charges against him to hold him for a while and that I would get a call if something changes and he is released. The girls and Tony and I went back to our home that was a crime scene, I didn't think to go before them to clean up, I wasn't thinking at all. I was just in a haze of disbelief. When we got in the door I ran up to shut my bedroom door before the girls saw anything upsetting. All of the bedding and my clothes that I had on were gone along with the gun cabinet placed in evidence.

Once again, trying to bring a routine back to our home without Mark, I went into work. Most of the staff had heard by this time because Angie and Tanya said something. I had several looks of pity and a long meeting with my boss. After I got out of the meeting, Sherrie grabbed me and had me come in her office. She wrote me a check for five thousand dollars and made an appointment with her lawyer for that afternoon. I would pay her back over time but she wanted me to get out before Mark finishes the job. I called Terry and had her meet me at the lawyer's office, I needed a second set of ears to hear what I wasn't able to process.

An hour and a half later, the papers were drawn up and Mark was served his divorce papers in jail where they could not be refused. That would be the beginning of a long drawn out divorce. Terry and I left the lawyers and went to the grocery store to get some dinner stuff for the kids and I. The checker looked at me and said my card was declined. I don't know how that could have been because I hadn't had time to spend any money since the Friday before. I called the bank to find out what the problem was with the account. Mark had cleaned our accounts out, there was nothing. I didn't have a dime to my name. My own paycheck was in his hands because it took a few weeks to complete the change account paperwork with the school district. My paycheck was deposited into the joint account and was gone, all of it, gone. I started sobbing, I didn't know what to do, how to get by without any money for at least a month, which would be after Christmas. Terry paid for the groceries and took me home, she was having to pick up the pieces.

We were unloading the grocery bags through the garage and I noticed some things were out of place. Someone had been in my garage and I knew it wasn't Mark because he was locked up. I looked up to the ceiling and saw the door to our attic was ajar. I grabbed the latter and climbed up there to have a look. All of the gifts that we had bought for the family and the kids were gone, they had been stolen. Now I had no money and no gifts for my kids, I don't know how he was doing it, but Mark was paying me back from behind bars.

I reached out to the detective to notify them of the theft. It would be something they made a note of but couldn't do anything about unless I had an idea of who might have gone into the garage. Terry was right there to help me out again and volunteered to buy a few little things for me to give the kids on Christmas morning so they would have something form me to open. I was sure they were going to get all of the gifts I had already purchased, it would just appear they were coming from their father.

Just when I thought things couldn't get any more complicated than they already were, I got a call from the detective. Mark had been released on bail money that his family got together, I was told there was a restraining order on Mark and to call 911 if I even got a call from him. He was being released into the custody of his mother and would be staying there. I didn't say anything to the kids, I knew they would want to see him and I wasn't ready for that, I knew he would be trying to turn them against me. He was an unfit father in my book and I wasn't going to let him get his hands on any of them. I told Markie to stay at the dorm for his own safety that coming weekend, he didn't ask any questions, he just did what I asked. Markie had his own safe house and he was happy right where he was.

Tony was the first to hear from Mark and rushed down to see him. He also was the first to turn on me. He tolerated me during the school day but stayed with Mark at his grandma's because he didn't want him to be alone. Noel was next to hear from Mark, she had a cell phone so he could contact her whenever he wanted. Both girls were still somewhat in the dark about all of the details of that night but they asked to see him, I allowed this as long as Tony was with them, but only for small periods of time.

The next Friday I was at work trying to focus on anything accept the divorce and the holidays. I got a call that was forwarded to me from one of the other secretaries. It was Mark, he called to tell me he was going to kill himself and hoped that I was happy with myself. He was hysterically crying, I told him I would be hanging up and calling the police. He threatened to come after me if I did. I hung up, called the detective in charge of my case. He told me to get out of town, it wasn't safe until Mark was locked up again. They were in the middle of building their case, several felony charges were being tallied for the final hit on Mark. The upside to be part of a felony case, I am always excused from jury duty.

That night, Terry drove the girls and I up to my niece's place in the mountains. She was working as an accountant for one of the ski resorts and Mark would not find us there. It was only for a couple of days but much needed, I haven't felt safe for months. I needed the break because when I returned, I would be facing Mark in court. I hadn't seen him since Black Friday.

The End and the Beginning

The break at my niece's place was not long enough for the bruises to fade, on some level they will always be visible to me. Even when no one else could see them to speculate what I had been through, I could feel the colors burning through my skin. Shades of blues and greens, then that God awful yellow color that just won't go away with any amount of makeup. Once again, I found myself having to take a deep breath and keep my head up.

A court date the week of Christmas was not my idea of festive, but it is when we were appointed by the courts to appear. I asked Jack to go with me to court, Terry has been so supportive, but I needed the muscle behind me on this day, I was afraid Mark would try something and I didn't want to face that alone. My lawyer was a real bulldog and fought with the best of them, but she was a petite, buxom, blond woman who couldn't physically hurt a fly.

The three of us walked in the courtroom together, I was in the middle, with the lawyer on one side and Jack on the other. I almost got sick right there in my seat when I saw Mark and his lawyer walk in the room. I couldn't concentrate on anything that was being said and had to be briefed after the judge excused us. The general gist of what happened was that Mark and I had to be in a separation period for ninety days and then the papers would be filed and I would be free. In that three-month period, we would have to each complete a parenting class, which I am sure he needed. Along with a mediation to split all of our assets. That was a joke to me, we were in so much debt we had no assets. The mediation was set for after the holidays, this allowed the lawyers enough time to gather information on our financial situation. Prior to the divorce we were going to file bankruptcy, with the divorce pending we were instructed to not file bankruptcy and to short sell our house to avoid credit issues. I agreed to these terms and so did Mark at the time. The last thing I remember hearing was Mark laughing as loud as possible about how his kids would love the presents I had picked out for them on Black Friday. I found out later, my suspicions were confirmed about his brother Steve breaking into the attic and stealing the gifts for Mark. Steve never was held accountable for his actions, no one in that family ever managed to be truly punished for their actions.

Christmas Eve was always a time spent with Mark's side of the family. I allowed all of the kids to go with Mark to his grandmother's house for dinner but requested they be back no later than ten that night. I wasn't sure what was going to happen and I was still living in constant fear of Mark, I came up with a new tradition of putting our sleeping bags in front of the tree and waiting for Santa. They were all asleep in minutes, even the boys. This was an emotional time for all of us, that is one night I will always hold dear to my heart, for just a brief few hours, my babies were back and they were all mine. Christmas morning, I had a few things in the stockings and some random gifts that my sister had wrapped up and put my name on for the kids. I told them not to worry, they would be getting nice gifts when they saw their father. I never told them how he ended up with those gifts, I for the most part was a firm believer in not talking bad about the other parent. At the end of the day, negative parents can't help their children become better people. If only their father would have felt the same way about parenting.

New Year's Eve was anticlimactic, the boys went out and the girls stayed with friends. I found myself alone and I didn't like it, so I called up Terry and went to her house. Jack's brothers and sisters were over celebrating the start of a new year. I wasn't sure if I was up for celebrating so I decided to go home. I had this feeling of limbo where I didn't fit in anywhere with anyone, it was a horrible depressing feeling so I went to bed hoping I would wake up and things would look better on the first morning of a new year.

I still had a week off of work which allowed me to try to get much of the legal meetings and classes wrapped up. I am sure my boss was getting tired of the amount of work I was missing or my lack of presence even when I was physically in the office. I met with the layer, she went over all of the things we would be requesting at the mediation. We set the appointment for that meeting, I would have an assigned police officer outside the door to protect me from Mark. The restraining order wasn't going away until Mark completed all of the requirements of the court. Mark had not even appeared in court on charges at this point, I was trying very hard to get out of the marriage and he was trying very hard to avoid dealing with the real matter of his abuse.

I completed my parenting class and learned many valuable things. I was assigned to take the kids. They also had to complete a class with other kids going through the same thing with their parents. Tony had to go but would not go with me, he was leaning more and more towards Mark. I knew better than to argue with Tony, I would have to let him find out for himself what kind of man his father could be. I actually liked the class, it was informative and taught me the lesson of dealing with the lack of control I would have any time my kids were with their father, just as he had no control of the kids when they were with me. I could check that requirement off the list, now only mediation and then a few weeks until I was truly free of Mark.

The bulldog, my armed guard and I walked into the conference room of the mediation. Across the table sat Mark and his lawyer. On each end were the mediators, a husband and wife team put in place to help angry couples settle their financial differences outside of court. Unfortunately, they weren't dealing with rational people, one irrational person in this instance.

We sat there bickering back and forth about the most ridiculous things in our house. Mark spoke out of turn and insisted, "You take the car hauler trailer, I refuse to be caught with that in my possession!" I immediately brought to the groups attention that this was a trailer he had stolen a few years back to load his bikes and four wheelers to and from camping trips. I refused to take anything of his especially if it was stolen. Two hours after walking in that room, nothing had been solved. Mark was furious with his lawyer and fired him right in front of all of us. Mark would be representing himself here on out, I found that cause to celebrate. I was escorted to my jeep by the guard and off I went. It was time to wait for the court date of how all of our personal items and debt would be split.

My lawyer was on the phone setting a court date before she walked out of the mediation. I would meet with her another time to finalize requests and go over a game plan on what my future would look like. I really liked her as a person, until I got that bill, very eye opening to have to pay for friendship. If she got the job done, the money I owed would all be worth it.

The holidays and my time off were over, but my battle had not even truly started. The judge ruled in my favor for the most part, I had full parental rights of Noel and Morgan until they were old enough to decide they wanted to be with their father. Mark had visitation on Wednesdays and every other weekend. Tony chose to live with Mark full time but I still would see him at school every day. Our debt was split down the middle, not including the pending foreclosure of the house, we each walked away owing seventy-five thousand dollars. I agreed to give Mark everything in the garage, along with all of the vehicles and dirt bikes as long as I got to keep my jeep and the furniture in the house. In return for all of those things that Mark could sell for a decent amount, I asked for half of his retirement. I was hopeful because that would be a nice little chunk of change that I would be able to use to buy a new place or reinvest. Mark was assigned to a child services agent to go over what child support he would have to pay me monthly. Mark quit his job that day, he would get away with making money off the sale of his drugs under the table and leave me the expense of taking care of the kids.

Shortly after divorce court was complete, Mark started his hearings for all of the charges against him. There were so many, Mark found a different lawyer to represent him for that case. I hardly think Mark the Esquire would be able to negotiate for himself in that situation. Felony charges ranged from attempted murder with a concealed weapon (his hands were considered the weapon), rape, avoiding arrest, weapons and drug charges. The list went on and on, his lawyer accepted a deal for all of those things. If the district attorney would change some of the charges to misdemeanors, Mark would take a sentence of a year in jail, countless hours of community service, and punitive damages. Mark had to pay for all of the therapy the kids and I would be needing over the next year along with the bills that the city and county paid for while I was trying to find a place to live. Mark would end up owing thousands of dollars because I intended on using every resource offered to my family.

Legal battles take a very long time to see through, for the time being, Mark was not in jail, nor was he helping out with any of the bills the kids were racking up. It was February already and between orthodontist and general doctor appointments, I could hardly keep up. Every night when I come home from work, I would pull up to a neon pink paper taped to my garage door. The eviction was coming, I only had a few months left before I would lose our home for good, unless we could do a short sale. Either way, the girls and I were moving and I didn't have a dime to my name. Every penny I earned went to legal fees or my loan that I always paid back to Shelly on time. Along with just trying to feed the girls and keep them in their sports, I was strapped.

Terry had come up with an idea that would benefit her family and mine. I had asked before to sell my third of our family cabin. Terry and Jack didn't have the funds to buy me out and my brother would want to be bought out too which meant double the price. These were desperate times and I needed a lot of money to bail myself out of debt, the little left over would help me move once the house was sold. The sale of my portion wasn't enough to save my house, but it was enough to save my ass. This process took a few weeks but would be the answer to my prayers when I did get the funds. Mark could not touch this money because this cabin was mine before he and I were married. There was light at the end of my tunnel, maybe a little light but big enough to give me hope.

While waiting for my big windfall to hit, I still had to keep providing and surviving. Terry had found an organization that helped people in need. I couldn't believe that was my new title but if it helped to put food on the table I would embrace it. I was able to bring twenty dollars to a church up the hill once a month and get all of the main staples of the house to keep the kids from starving. I wish I was making that up, but there were many nights that I would run over and get the leftovers that Terry's family was done with to feed the kids. I would lay awake at night and wonder how it seemed like just yesterday that I was a happy and spoiled twelve-year-old girl who wanted for nothing. Now a middle aged single mom unable to put food on the table of the home that we would be leaving.

I would cry myself to sleep at night, Noel and Morgan couldn't stand hearing me, they started taking turns sleeping with me so that I wouldn't be alone. I couldn't have made it through those nights without them by my side. I would reassure them that things were going to get better and I would find a new fun place for us to live. I said it out loud for them and to convince myself that was the truth.

Every day I would do anything to avoid looking in the mailbox at the stack of bills. One afternoon I went out and grabbed the mail to find a speeding ticket addressed to Markie. I called him that minute and started to ream him about speeding and according to location not being in classes. Markie swore to me that he had not gotten a ticket and it must be a mistake because according to the date of the ticket, he was in Florida at a wrestling tournament and his car was parked at the house. I apologized to him and informed him that I would call the police station to find out how such a ticket would have been given.

Instead of calling the police station directly, I decided to ask the officer who was part of the school staff for security to have a look at the ticket. I gave him the ticket to take to the station. I was told the ticket would have fingerprints of the driver on the bottom of the page. The officer ran the prints in the data base and low and behold, they belonged to Tony. I was at a loss, Tony still had not taken care of his classes or fines from the violation of over a year ago. I asked my friend what we do next? I didn't like the answer I got back in this case. If I let Markie take the speeding ticket and add it to his record, it would possibly jeopardize his scholarship. If I turned Tony in to the police for impersonation, he would have a felony charge added to his other legal issues.

I had to make a choice that no mother ever wants to make, but I had to have Tony be accountable for his actions. It wasn't fair to Markie to be punished for the mistakes that Tony was making all of the time. I asked the school officer to arrest Tony, he was kind enough to wait until class was over. Tony left with the officer and got in the back of the car, no handcuffs needed to avoid drama at the school. It would take a few hours for Tony to be booked, this gave me enough time to get in touch with a bail bond person because I didn't have the money to get him out.

I met the woman who was in charge of the bail money at the jail, we went in and bailed Tony out but under the bond name. It was up to me to make sure Tony went to his court hearings or I would be responsible for paying the money back, that was not an option. Having Tony arrested pushed him further away from me and closer to his father. I knew it would happen, but it was in everyone's best interest to take care of this the right way.

I waited for a few hours outside the jail, because it was a nice day and the inside gave me the creeps. The people waiting to visit their loved ones quite possibly were just as disturbing as the people locked up. I realize that sounds very judgmental, I just wasn't sure how to sit next to a mother who had kids with her and tear drop tattoos on the side of her face. I gladly waited outside on a bench, not in peace because the inmates that had access to windows would pound on them to get the attention of anyone outside. The experience is one that I would love to forget, but instead would become very used to after sentencing.

Tony finally walked out with a very angry look on his face, I have seen that look before on Mark's face. His golden eyes turned dark and stormy as he glared at me as if looks could truly kill. It was heart breaking to be seeing that hateful look on the face of my boy, a boy I raised as best as I could. Tony demanded to be dropped off with his father. As I drove away I wondered if they would eventually share the same cell.

I arrived home to a big empty house, the girls were both at basketball practice for another hour and had rides home. It seemed like a good time to take a nice hot bath in my custom whirlpool that would only be available to me until the eviction. It took longer than I thought to start my relaxing bath because Morgan liked to let her turtle go swimming in the tub before she waxed it for the day. That meant either a scrub brush and disinfectant or a shower in my bathroom. I went with the shower.

After I was all nice and pruned up, I put my pajamas on and crawled into bed. This was the same bed I almost died in, I thought somehow putting new sheets and comforter on the top would take away from the memories, but they always came flooding back. I started to cry then my phone rang and made me swallow my tears and move on for the moment. I had been talking with my first boyfriend from high school again. We reconnected through Face Book and thought we would get together and catch up. We chatted for a while before my girls came home and made a plan for the upcoming weekend. Noel and Morgan would be at their grandmother's seeing their father so it wouldn't upset them. I wasn't ready to tell them I was going out with another man. Mark had started sleeping with anything and everything and flaunting it in front of all of the kids, I decided I would not be sharing my personal life with any of them until I found the right person to introduce them to. I wanted to protect them from getting to know a person and having them disappear the next day, it's just not my style.

That weekend I got dressed up to meet for dinner, we talked for hours about all of the things we had been through over the last twenty years. I was fourteen when I fell for Jeff and so much had changed. I thought there would be some spark left between us. I was willing to find out, it gave me comfort to have someone to talk to but I kept most of my secrets to myself. I didn't need anyone to know the troubles I was going through with Tony or the way Mark and I ended. I still wasn't ready to deal with all of that and I certainly wasn't ready to answer questions or defend myself.

We went out on a few more dates, but Jeff was a good Catholic and wasn't planning to take our relationship to the bedroom until I was officially divorced. I still had a few weeks of the separation to power through before the papers were signed. I was not thrilled with his devotion to the church I am Catholic to, but I am also human. I would leave in my jeep after every date wondering if he would eventually crack.

While I not so patiently waited for Jeff to come around to new age thinking, I made arrangements for the girls and I to fly to California to visit my brother and his family. More like, they paid for the tickets and insisted that I get out of town for a while to decompress from all of the trauma. I was more than happy to run away to San Diego, it's where I always felt at home. I still run away as often as I can, it is the coming home that becomes harder and harder.

My family has always pampered me when I am out to visit and they spared no expense this go around for the girls and I. We went to Sea World and out to eat along with all of the other sightseeing

135

things that tourists do. I was able to relax knowing I didn't have to look over my shoulder all of the time waiting for the other shoe to drop. We were only there for a long weekend but it gave the girls and I a chance to splurge a bit because we hadn't been doing anything for ourselves. I am grateful to have supportive family. The one piece of advice my brother left me with from that trip was to try everything once and not to fear the unknown. Easier said than done, but I keep pushing myself to do new things even if they are only worth trying once.

The second we landed my anxiety returned, I would make an appointment to see my new therapist this week. I needed some new coping skills to deal with everything that I was avoiding while I was laying on the beach in California. One relief was the closing of my portion of the cabin would be soon, I would be able to pay down my debt and start looking for a place for the girls and I. I called the company that Mark's retirement was held with and asked to withdraw my half. I was told I was going to lose my half if I didn't file the proper legal documents.

Another panic attack and a phone call to my lawyer before finding out that her assistant had failed to file those documents and I would have to pay another five thousand dollars to have them drawn up and delivered. I called the investment company back to ask if there was a way around this process and why am I just now being told that I might not have any money. Mark had made a withdraw of as much as he could, thinking he would keep me from my share. He almost succeeded had I not called to find out how much I was going to be receiving. Fortunately, the company had received the divorce papers and held my half for thirty days before releasing it to Mark. I fired my lawyer and drew up the paperwork, then had the courthouse notarize and send on my behalf. It didn't cost me anything and I was still going to get my money. The catch, not until Mark turns fifty or dies whichever comes first.

The thought crossed my mind, but I wouldn't be able to live with myself if I was in some way responsible for the death of my children's father, not that I had any control over the fate of Mark's existence. No child should go through what I had lived through when my father was taken from me as a child. Morgan was only ten, she had the right to grow up with a father, it would be his fault if she grew up to hate him. Mark was well on his way to festering those feelings with my daughters.

We were reminded of just how bad of a person Mark is one night when pulling into the drive after practices. The girls and thought it would be another late dinner rush through homework night. It was until there was a loud knock on the door. I am not a fan of opening the door after dark because you never know what you will get on the other side. Tonight, I answered the door to a man who claimed that Mark owed him money for some lighting equipment that was used at his other house to grow marijuana.

Mark had to give up the other house to save face through all of his court hearings and legal issues. I have no idea where any of the stuff in that house went, but this guy wanted his lights back or the drugs owed to him. Noel came curiously to the door and stood behind me, I pushed her back and told her to get Uncle Jack to get over here right away. She could tell my tone of voice meant danger. The man was threatening us to stop hiding Mark and to have him come out and settle up. There was some deal between the two of them that Mark would use the lighting system in exchange for drugs. This very large intimidating man was a drug dealer and wasn't taking my word that I had not seen Mark in weeks. I pleaded with him to understand our circumstances, just as he was ready to push through the door, Jack pulled up. He got out of his truck and asked what the problem was? The man didn't flinch until Jack mentioned the cops would be arriving any minute. Apparently, that is all I needed to do to scare him away, what a fool I was to think I could rationalize with a criminal.

Just another reminder of how I needed a fresh start, maybe losing the house was the best thing for my family. I knew the time was drawing near to sign the papers and move out of our home, I wanted to get as much money as I could for all of the things that I had settled for in the divorce agreement. I set up a big garage sale for the coming weekend to squeeze those pennies. There was no way we would be able to take everything in the house, I would have to dramatically downsize into a smaller townhome or apartment. I had started looking but had not committed to anything because I wanted to take as much time as I could sorting through things and packing.

During the garage sell I was notified that Mark had been arrested. I no longer had to keep track of his court dates and he didn't bother to keep up with the specifics. He was picked up on a warrant for not appearing on all of the charges from our horrendous ending. This time he would not be getting out, Mark was sentenced to a year and he was starting his time when the law saw fit. I explained to all of the kids that it was time for their father to pay for his mistakes. They knew it was coming but didn't want to acknowledge it until they had to.

Tony remained at his grandmother's house, the girls and I continued to pack, and Markie was still up at school. Nothing changed other than where they had to visit their father. I refused to take the girls so Tony and Markie would when they were able to. Mark could only have three visitors at a time so someone always had to stay back, I let the kids decide who was going and when. I was sleeping again and Mark's visitation schedule didn't concern me one bit. The only visit I was interested in was the one with my realtor. We were ready to short sale the house, I just needed Mark's signatures and then I would be able to move and maintain some dignity. Mark was not about to let me have my dignity or make things easier for his children. Sitting in jail reading through the papers, Mark sent them back through the guard to the realtor. He didn't sign them, he told the realtor he would rather see me evicted and out on the streets than to make my life any easier.

Mark didn't realize I had sold my share of the cabin and we would be moving into a different place with or without his signature.

What he did do was cause his daughters plenty of embarrassment the day the Sheriff came to remove us from our home. As soon as Mark didn't sign the papers I went and rented a place close to the school and my work. I was afraid the eviction would ruin my chances of getting anything because it would go against my credit for the next seven years. When the Sheriff arrived we were ready, the stuff we wanted was already at the new place. The girls and I cried as we walked out of the house for the last time.

The new place was smaller, but each girl still had her own room. I was unpacking and cleaning to make it feel more like home. I took them shopping to pick out new bedding to spruce up their rooms. None of these things were working because it didn't feel like home. I was more irritated with myself for leaving the vacuum at the other house than I was losing the house. In hindsight if life would have played out different, I would still have my Dyson and my girls would still be home. That just isn't how it worked out and now we had to make the best of things. It was almost summer break and we would be busy with softball tournaments and pool time at our new place, at least there was a pool.

The day had arrived for Mark and I to sign our divorce papers. I signed them the second I got them in my hot little hands. I was sure Mark would sign them because he was busy trying to play the victim sitting in jail because of me. I still held my breath, he signed them but not without stating that someday he would make me pay. I guess the twenty years that I was paying wasn't enough.

Terry was so thrilled that the divorce was final she offered to throw me a divorce party. Angie was going to help her plan the big event with Terry. All I had to do was show up in a new dress. The party would be held a few days after Tony's graduation. I felt that was the big celebration that needed attention. He was going to make it, I was very proud that he managed to stay the course with all of the commotion in his life. As proud of Tony as I was for completing high school, I knew in my heart the much more challenging roads were ahead. Tony had to want to get clean and as of late, he was asking strictly for money for graduation. I knew better and had spread the word to my family to only give gifts or gift cards to stores. Mark's family gave him money, they may as well have handed him the drugs.

The ceremony was memorable with baby pictures of Tony and a little blurb of what he wanted to do with the rest of his life. Like all of the students that struggled to graduate, they created the idea that they were going to all move on to bigger and better things in the future. It's exactly what every parent wants to hear in that moment. I had a get together for Tony after the graduation to show him how much I support and love him. I think that all of the kids needed reminding of that, but Tony mostly needed to know someone was in his corner. He seemed lost without his father around.

The graduation celebrations had come to an end and it was time for me to be the bell of the ball again, this time for my endings. Terry and Angie had arranged to reserve the back room of Baker's Street Pub since I would want to be there hanging out anyway. This time I got to do it with my family and friends. My kids were not there, this was not a celebration to them and Terry thought to keep it quiet. So many of my friends showed up and gave me encouragement to move forward and that I had done the right thing even if it didn't feel like it where the kids were concerned. Terry warned me to only do nine shots and no more. I got a chuckle out of that, I am not sure what the significance of nine meant to her, maybe that is all she could stomach. I think I had put away about a dozen by the end of the night, but I have a higher tolerance than Terry where alcohol is concerned.

Not just friends and family were at the bar, we only had a small section reserved. The bar was packed and the music was awesome. All 80's tunes, it just worked out that way but I thanked Terry and Angie as if they had pulled some magic string to make the night perfect.

The weather was just right. It was a warm night in early summer, and I had just a touch of color from lying by the pool with Noel and Morgan earlier that day. I was soaking the attention up and was feeling no pain. I was standing by the door getting ready to go out to the patio to mingle with friends when I saw a blast from the past. Standing there in the doorway looking at me with crystal blue eyes was the boy I once called my best friend. I hadn't seen him in twenty years and my heart stopped right there. He looked as shocked to see me as I was to see him, he had grown and I mean in a good way. We chatted for a minute and then exchanged numbers to hang out some time. It sounded cliché at the time. He left and I continued to enjoy the lime light until it was closing time.

Two days later I got a call, it was him asking to meet for a drink. How could I say no? We met at Old Chicago, I still remember what he was wearing. Jeans, flip flops, and a Lake Powell shirt it was enough to send me over the moon. I kept my drink limit to only two because I wanted to have my wits about me, I could have easily gone home with him, but I was portraying the less than interested woman. Just friends, until he walked me to my jeep and kissed me like no man has ever done before.

I wondered to myself, could this be the one, the love of my life? Only time will tell.

Printed in the United States
By Bookmasters